Death By Greed

A Josiah Reynolds Mystery
Book Eighteen

Abigail Keam

Worker Bee Press

Book cover by Cricket Press.
Edited by Penny Baker.
Author's photograph by Peter Keam.

Special thanks to Melanie Murphy and Liz Hobson.

ISBN 978 1 953478 12 2
31423

Published in the USA by

Worker Bee Press
P.O. Box 485
Nicholasville, KY 40340

Books By Abigail Keam

The Josiah Reynolds Mysteries
Death By A HoneyBee I
Death By Drowning II
Death By Bridle III
Death By Bourbon IV
Death By Lotto V
Death By Chocolate VI
Death By Haunting VII
Death By Derby VIII
Death By Design IX
Death By Malice X
Death By Drama XI
Death By Stalking XII
Death By Deceit XIII
Death By Magic XIV
Death By Shock XV
Death By Chance XVI
Death By Poison XVII
Death By Greed XVIII
Death By Theft XVIX

The Mona Moon Mystery Series
Murder Under A Blue Moon I
Murder Under A Blood Moon II
Murder Under A Bad Moon III
Murder Under A Silver Moon IV
Murder Under A Wolf Moon V
Murder Under A Black Moon VI
Murder Under A Full Moon VII
Murder Under A New Moon VIII
Murder Under A British Moon IX
Murder Under A Bridal Moon X
Murder Under A Western Moon XI
Murder Under A Honey Moon XII

1

I was working my bees when I heard a thunderous bellowing and smashing of wood. Baby, my English Mastiff, took off like a rocket to a neighboring field, barking and growling. He repeatedly ran back to me as if saying "Are you coming? Are you coming?"

Jumping into my golf cart, I followed Baby to one of my horse pastures where I was stunned to see an enormous Texas Longhorn bawling out his poor, anguished heart. Frightened and angry, this behemoth had broken through my horse fence and was now snorting and tossing his head in protest at Comanche, a valuable breeding stallion rearing and neighing in fear and rage himself.

I was beside myself as I had given up boarding Thoroughbred stallions because they proved to be ill-tempered. Comanche had been moved next door to Lady Elsmere's farm but temporarily relocated back with me as his pasture was being re-seeded.

The sight of Comanche tossing his mane and slashing the air with his dangerous hooves did nothing to deter the bull, who lowered his horns. That bull could gut Comanche with one tip of his powerful horns. Comanche lunged and then sidestepped the bull at the last moment. The bull shook his head and roared, stomping the ground. The Thoroughbred's actions only incited the Longhorn to more fury. Both animals were a terrible sight to behold in their wrathful frenzy.

Oh, Lordy! What to do? What to do? I had never come across this situation before. Have you?

I knew the bull, feeling threatened would and could, with those long horns, spanning eight feet from tip to tip, kill that priceless Thoroughbred. The horse was my responsibility since he was back in my care. My friend had invested every penny she had in that horse. I shuddered at the thought of Comanche being injured and knew I had to rescue the ebony steed, but how?

I immediately ran into the stable for several buckets of sweet feed and hoisted the feed over the broken fence. I rapped the buckets on a fence post to create a distraction. "Hey, bully bull! Hey, you there, sonny! I got some tasty treats for you!"

The bull turned at the noise I was making, snorted, and pawed the ground. Now I'm not familiar with cattle behavior, but I am smart enough to realize that snorting, pawing, and lowering one's head means trouble in Texas Longhorn behavior 101. Sure enough, the bull charged—at me.

I ran screaming into the stable with Baby close on my heels. I slammed the stable doors shut and put up the cross bar. True to his nature, the bull rammed the doors and almost knocking them off their hinges. "Merde," I yelped. That's French for "manure", and I was deep in it at the moment.

Baby and I ran through the stable and out the other side. Now when I say run, that means a very fast walk for me as I limp with one leg and I am over fifty. Since Baby is a healthy English Mastiff, he left me high and dry. I don't blame him. Just wish I could run as fast as he.

I had to get help. Climbing over fences (not my strong suit), I managed to get to my neighbor, Lady Elsmere, where I could ask for assistance. I knew her farm manager, Mike, had a tranquilizer gun. As I ran, I could still hear the bull slamming his massive head against my stable doors. BOOM! BOOM!

Thank goodness he was preoccupied with tearing up the stable.

I hoped I had an intact barn left once we got the beast under control—if we got him under control.

I certainly didn't want to put that magnificent animal down.

2

My name is Josiah Reynolds and I'm a beekeeper living in the Kentucky Bluegrass—horse country. I make my living from selling honey at a local farmers' market. I also board horses and own a catering business. I rent out my home, the Butterfly, for events. The Butterfly is built from local timber, slate, and limestone. The entire back wall is glass so one can see for miles. It's perched on the edge of the Palisades which is a cliff system bordering the Kentucky River.

It was from this cliff that a rogue cop pushed me, causing my bad left leg and the need to wear a hearing aid. I shattered my teeth, fractured my jaw, and broke so many bones that I lost count. I should have died, but instead of falling one hundred feet to the river below, I landed on a ledge forty feet down hitting tree branches all the way. I made my way back to the land of the living after a long convalescence.

Before the accident, my husband left me for another woman and had a love child with her. That wasn't the worst of it. He stole my share of our assets, my good jewelry, and designer dresses, which he gave to his girlfriend. I managed to keep the farm, but lost my job as an art history professor on track to becoming the next dean in my department at a local university, due to the scandal and gossip. I should have sued.

I refused to give my lousy husband a divorce until he returned my possessions including my money, but he up and died, taking the secret location of our assets with him. I know he gave everything to his mistress. Just can't prove it. I was on the edge of bankruptcy for several years, but fought my way back to solvency. I have money in the bank now and have doubled the size of my farm. I still deal with physical pain, but it gets less every year.

The only odd thing is that after I recovered from my fall, I seem to stumble over dead bodies all the time. Seventeen so far. Bizarre—don't you think?

"Josiah, I'm talking to you," Mike said. "You drifted off."

"Oh, sorry. Was thinking about something else. What did you ask?"

"Do you want to try a cattle prod?"

"Does that animal look like a cattle prod will bother him? It will just enrage him further. I think a sedative is the most humane way of dealing with him."

"The problem is I don't know how much to give a Longhorn steer."

I bent over to take a peek and did a double-check. Yep, I had been right in the first place. "I think he is a bull."

Mike checked and then chuckled. "How could I have missed those?" he said, referring to the bull's obvious sexual prowess.

"Just wing it, Mike."

"Is there a safe place we can bed this handsome fellow until you find the owners?" Mike asked, putting a dart into the gun.

"We can put him in the front stall. It's large enough for his horns," I replied, gawking at the bellowing bull who now had one of his horns stuck through my stable door. "He'll be able to move around freely."

Now a horse stall is usually 12 x 12 feet. Mine were 14 x14 feet to accommodate the larger horse breeds, but I had one double stall that was 24 x 24 feet. That's where I decided to put him.

Mike ordered, "Fill his water bucket and put lots of hay and sweet feed in the stall. Once I shoot him, we only have a short time to work with him."

"How are we going to move that monster if he falls?"

"I'm just giving him enough tranquilizer to calm him. He'll stay on his feet, but we'll be able to work with him safely."

I replied, sarcastically, mind you, "Sure, Mike, anything you say." I tried not to roll my eyes. This was a dangerous job and I knew it. So did Mike.

"It would be easier to work with him if he had a nose ring."

I said, "The vet should be here soon."

"You want me to wait?"

"No. He's tearing up my barn, and I'm afraid he'll injure himself. I'll have the vet check him out when he gets here. He shouldn't be long." I filled the water bucket and put lots of feed into the stall before nodding to Mike. "I think we're ready."

"The vet should be able to give him more sedative so he can sleep off his hissy fit." Mike took aim and shot the dart into the bull, which bellowed and kicked. It caused him to push into the door, which finally snapped off its hinges. The bull now had part of a barn door hanging off his horn. He was free and rushed us.

Mike and I jumped into his truck. The Longhorn lowered his head and rammed the vehicle almost turning us over. The part of my barn door attached to his horn shattered, causing the noise to frighten the animal even more as he turned to take another run at us. I think I screamed, but I'm not sure. I just held on. Mike reloaded his gun with another dart, aimed through the open driver's side window, and shot the big guy in the shoulder as he was thundering toward us again.

The sedative worked fast this time. The bull stopped suddenly, blinked heavily, looked woozy, and started to go down. One of Lady Elsmere's farm workers ran up and put Styrofoam on the tips of the bull's horns and a blanket over his eyes. The other farm hands, which had been standing at a discreet distance, now ran over to push and pull the confused and dazed bull into the stall. The bull eased down onto his knees, sounding a thud.

Mike exited his truck and put another dart into the gun just in case. "He's good, Josiah. He's pretty doped up. I think it is safe."

Assured the bull was inside the stall, I got out of Mike's truck and went inside my damaged stable. "Check his breathing," I requested, observing the bull from outside the stall. "It looks a little labored."

Mike entered the stall and carefully moved the animal's head so the horns would not be obstructed when the Longhorn moved his head. He finally put a bale of hay under the bull's chin to keep the horns stable. They had to be heavy.

The bull gave one last hostile snort as a spasm shook its heavy bulk causing the men to run out of the stall. I slammed the stall door shut after them. I didn't like the angle of the bull's head as I didn't think cattle laid their heads like that, but I wasn't going into the stall to fix it. As I was calling the vet again, he pulled up in his van. I went out to meet him.

Esau Clay is his name and he's seen me through a number of "situations" with my critters. I must brag that Esau is a direct descendant of Henry Clay, the Great Compromiser who is considered one of the greatest statesmen the U.S. ever had. Henry Clay is also credited with bringing Kentucky bourbon to Washington D.C. and introducing the Mint Julep to his fellow congressmen at the Willard Hotel. Apparently, congressmen and senators would meet in the late afternoon at the hotel and drink a little nip or two before going home to dinner. Taking charge, Clay would make Mint Juleps from behind the bar. No wonder Henry Clay is called the Great Compromiser. He was getting his colleagues liquored up and sloppily agreeing to his proposals—I surmise. Kind of brilliant in a sleazy way.

"What is it this time, Josiah?" Esau asked, staring at the front of my mangled barn. He gawked at it curiously.

"That is the problem," I replied, thumbing at the barn.

"May I go in?"

"By all means, Esau." I followed the vet inside and stood back with Mike and the rest of the men in the aisle.

Esau looked aghast. "Good lord. How did this Longhorn get here?"

I asked, "Do you know him?"

"He belongs to a breeding facility in Madison County." Esau poked the bull through the stall slats and when the bull didn't respond except for a grunt, he went inside to examine the animal. "We gotta get this animal back on his feet first thing. I don't like his breathing."

"I didn't like his breathing either. You said you know this bull?"

"I do. His name is Tex, and I've treated him a couple of times."

"That's an original name for a Texas Longhorn," I commented, sardonically.

Mike asked, "Okay, but how did Tex get here?"

Esau replied, "I imagine he broke loose and swam across the river."

"Cattle can swim?" I asked.

As he examined the animal, Esau commented, "If they are desperate enough. This bull has been abused. He's got cattle prod burns all over him and bizarre scratches and cuts. He's in bad shape. I'm going to give him a shot of antibiotics and one for pain. Then I'm gonna wake him up. He needs to be up on his feet." Esau turned to me. "Can you keep him here until I see what's going on with the owner?"

"Sure, but will he be willing to stay? He can go right through that stall if he has a mind to."

"I'm going to give you pain pills and more sedative doses in a pill form to give Tex—just enough to take the edge off his fear. He should be calmer when he feels safe. Like I said, I've worked with this bull before.

He's actually gentle."

"Yeah, right." But once I heard that the animal had been mistreated, I knew my duty. Tex had to stay. No wonder he was tearing up the countryside. "Sure, I'll keep him here—for a little while."

Esau gave me a thumb up. "You're a good egg, Josiah."

"All I can say is 'no good deed goes unpunished.'"

"It will be fine. You'll see."

I didn't respond. I knew I was going to regret Tex staying in my barn, but what else could I do? I shrugged. "Whatever you say, Esau."

The vet turned to Mike's men. "Okay, gentlemen. Two men on the horns and the rest of you on the other side of me. When I say okay, let's get him up."

Neither Mike nor his crew looked very happy as they followed Esau's instructions, as he gave the creature antibiotic and pain medication before rubbing antibiotic cream on his wounds. Satisfied, Esau mumbled, "That should keep bacterial infections at bay. Now let's listen to his heart and lungs."

After the vet put his stethoscope away, I asked, "How is he?"

"His lungs sound a little ragged, but his heart is sound. Let's get him up on his feet. He should breathe better then." Esau administered a stimulant.

As soon as the bull began to stir, the vet yelled, "Okay!"

The five men pulled and pushed as the Longhorn struggled to get on his feet. The bull stood and quivered a bit before he went down again.

"Oh, dear," I said. "Now what?"

"He's coming out of the daze," the vet reassured. "He's a little wobbly but he'll come out of that soon. See, he's holding his head up. That's what we need to witness. He's already breathing better. Let's give him some peace and quiet. When Tex feels comfortable, he will stand. He's a little confused at the moment. When he drinks and eats, that's the sign that he's out of the danger zone."

"Gee, I wish I could give him all the quiet that monster needs, but Tex ripped the barn door off the hinges, so he'll have to put up with a little noise here and there. And Doc Clay, that stall is not going to keep that raging bovine contained."

"He'll be fine, Jo. He's already settling down."

I continued to protest. "Well, I'm not fine. Who's gonna pay for the damage to my barn and fence? Hey, where are you going?" I pursued Esau to his van.

"I'm going to notify the owner where his bull is and give him the riot act about the condition of that animal. If I don't get a good explanation, I'm gonna report him."

I jumped in the van with him. "I'm coming with you. I want an explanation, too. You can bring me back and check on Tex again."

The vet gave me a stern look. "Only if you let me do all the talking, and you behave."

"Who me? You're asking for the moon," I quipped, giving Esau a lopsided grin. I was determined to go and he knew it.

The vet sighed and reluctantly started his vehicle. He gave me one last glance of apprehension and gently shook his head before putting the van in drive.

We were on our way.

3

"Hello?" I called out.

We had gone to the owner's two-story brick house, but no one answered when we rang the bell. I tried the doors, but they were locked. The owner's dually truck was hitched to a large trailer parked in the driveway, so we knew the owner had to be somewhere near. We ventured to the breeding facility, where Esau and I both shouted for the owner.

"Hello?" I hollered again.

"Ulysses, are you here?" Esau cried out.

"Ulysses?" I muttered.

"His full name is Ulysses Grant."

"You jest."

"I'm serious and you promised to behave."

"Did I?"

"Ulysses is touchy about his name, so no cracks. He might make one about your moniker."

"I'll have you know that my John Hancock was bestowed upon me by my grandmother, who named me after a righteous king from the Old Testament."

"Funny how it didn't take. The righteous part I mean."

"Oh, ha ha. So hilarious." I pushed deeper into the barn and was alarmed at what I witnessed. "Esau, this doesn't look right."

Following behind me, Esau commented "Everything is all torn up. Looks like Tex's meltdown started here."

I looked about the scattered straw on the floor, tools in disarray, broken stall doors, feed sacks torn apart. "I thought this was a breeding facility. Where are the rest of the animals?"

Concerned, Esau said, "That's a good question, Jo. I'm going to look in the pastures. Can you check the rest of the barn?"

"Sure."

Esau handed me a walkie-talkie and turned it on. "Use this. The reception is not good out here for phones. Very spotty. Call me if you find anything."

"Okay," I replied, sticking the walkie-talkie in my vest pocket.

Esau left and I ventured deeper into this large metal facility. Esau called it a barn, but it looked like it was more than that. There were about thirty stalls that I could see and all sorts of cubicles and locked storage areas. The concrete floor was strewn with discarded hay and straw. Hay is feed for the animals, and straw is used for bedding.

I found a cattle prod on the floor and picked it up, as I didn't know what I was going to run into. As I pressed on the switch, it worked—electricity crackled from its prongs. I wondered if it had been used on my newly-acquired Texas Longhorn.

The facility gave me the creeps. The metal barn was unusually quiet except for rock doves flying about the rafters, and it smelled of fly-riddled manure, urine, and filthy bedding combined with the strong scent of molasses. The barn was not sanitary and hadn't been cleaned for a long time. Looking inside some of the stalls, I noticed the water was low in dirty buckets, and some of the feed smelled moldy. I was already taking a dislike to this Ulysses fellow.

I made my way through the main corridor of the facility until I came to what looked like an office. "Ulysses! Mr. Grant," I called out, as I hurried toward it. "This is Josiah Reynolds. I've got your bull. I've got Tex." I stopped suddenly. Oh, no. This was not good.

The cheap office door was ajar with a foot sticking out. I visually followed the foot to legs that led to a torso that led to a head. It was the body of an older man dressed in a blue-checkered shirt and worn-out jeans. One black boot was missing. Congealed blood pooled out from beneath him. I knew it was useless, but I bent over, feeling for a pulse. I pulled my hand back in a flash. The body was cold.

Pulling out the walkie-talkie, I said, "Esau. Esau!"

"Yeah, over."

"I think I found Ulysses Grant. He's dead. Over."

"I'll be right there. Don't touch anything. Over."

I righted an overturned bale of hay and sat down, pondering—why me? Why did I have to stumble upon dead people? It was unnerving. This was my eighteenth corpse.

Dead people were the gift that kept on giving.

4

The police came. An ambulance came. The coroner came. The photographer came. The forensic crew came. Finally a homicide detective from the nearest town came. He said some cuss words when he stepped in a pile of manure and caught us staring at him. "Who are you?" he snapped at Esau and me sitting forlornly on several square bales of hay. I swear I felt fleas jumping on me.

"I'm Esau Clay. This is Josiah Reynolds."

"And why are you here messing up my crime scene?" The man's gaze flicked over us for a second. He was whip-thin with heavy-lidded eyes. He reminded me of a Tootsie Roll—brown hair, tanned skin, brown suit, dark shirt, and brown shoes with brown socks.

"We found the body," Esau replied, looking surprised. "Has no one told you?"

The man gave us a humorless smile. "I'm not sure why I'm here as the coroner said the man was gored. Can you shed some light on this?"

Esau and I glanced at each other.

"We think a Texas Longhorn escaped from this facility and ended up on Mrs. Reynolds' farm. We came to tell Ulysses that she had his bull," Esau answered.

"Is this bull dangerous?"

I asked, "What is your name, sir? We like to know whom we are speaking with."

"You're speaking to someone who knows better than to end a sentence with a preposition," rasped the Tootsie Roll man. "It should be—we like to know to whom we are speaking?"

I shot back, "It was good enough for Winston Churchill. 'This is the type of arrant pedantry I will not put up with.'" You know how I hate men correcting me.

"But that is not what Churchill said. 'This is the type of arrant pedantry up with which I will not put.'"

I replied, "It was tongue-in-cheek because the sentence sounded stilted without a preposition at the end."

Esau appeared astounded. "Hello. Let's get back to Ulysses Grant. I have sick animals waiting on me, and I need to get back to my practice." He shook his head. "Squabbling about Winston Churchill and prepositions. Yikes, you two."

The Tootsie Roll man looked contrite. "Sorry, my name is Detective McCain, Lucas McCain. I am working as a consultant on the case because this podunk little community doesn't have anyone trained in homicide investigation—thus, moi."

"We gave our statements."

"So I've been told."

"Is this a homicide?" I asked.

"The corner thinks it was an animal attack. If he confirms it, then it will be ruled as death by an animal assault or misadventure. We'll see. If I need for you to answer any more questions, I have your addresses and phone numbers. You may go."

"Thank you," Esau replied, helping me to my feet.

McCain asked, "You say you have this man's bull?"

Before Esau could answer, I said, "I've got a stray bull, but we don't know for sure if Mr. Grant owned it. That's why we came—to find out."

"You couldn't have called?"

I replied, "No one was picking up, and we didn't know if he had a landline. The number was not listed."

Esau added, "I had only his cell phone number. Like Mrs. Reynolds said, no one was picking up."

"Hmm," the detective said. "Your name seems awfully familiar to me, Mrs. Reynolds or is it Miss?" He leaned closer to eyeball me. "Have we met before?"

What he was really asking is if I had been previously arrested by him.

Esau jumped in. "Mrs. Reynolds is often in the society column." He didn't want Detective McCain to associate me with other murders, fearful the detective wouldn't let us leave.

"Huh," the detective muttered, still giving me an inquisitive glare. "Okay, you can go."

Esau grabbed my arm and dragged me out of the barn. He pushed me into his van and helped strap me in.

"I can do this myself," I said, pushing Esau's hands away. "I'm not an invalid—yet."

Esau hurried to the other side and got in. He turned on the ignition and sped out of there.

"What's wrong, Esau?"

"If Tex gored Ulysses, the authorities will order the animal to be euthanized."

"Maybe they should."

"I'm telling you that bull is gentle. If Tex did gore Ulysses, it's because the animal was traumatized. You saw the condition he was in."

"Actually, I didn't get that close to Tex, but I'll take your word for it."

"He is undernourished, burned, and bruised. I think someone beat him. Like humans, animals have the right to protect themselves against an aggressor. What would you do if someone treated Baby like that?"

"I see your point."

"Josiah, I want you to promise that you will do everything in your power to protect Tex."

"I don't know, Esau. He seems too much for me to handle. I know nothing about cattle. To be honest, he really scares me."

"Will you, at least, protect him while I look for another place for him?"

"That I'll do, but you'll take him off my hands soon. I mean next week."

"I promise, but I want you to do another favor for me."

"Yeah?" I looked at Esau suspiciously.

"I found other animals. They were stuck in a pasture and they, too, are in poor shape. You've got those additional pastures since you purchased the farm next door. They need a safe place to heal. Your farm is near my practice, so I can easily check on them. I can't just leave them here. There's no one to take care of them."

I shook my head. "No, Esau. No. No. No. I'm not going to get more involved, and I mean it." I did really mean it, too.

Esau just nodded and grinned. The next day, he showed up with a trailer of rare goats, sheep, and cattle.

I ask you—how do I get sucked into these things?

5

"I don't want to hear you complain, Josiah," Esau said as he led out a group of Valais Blacknose sheep. "I've helped you in the past. Now you return the favor."

"Who is gonna pay for their upkeep and feed? These animals are not my responsibility."

Esau shut the gate to the pasture. "Look at them, Jo. Aren't they the cutest things you've ever seen?"

The sheep were very sweet. They had little black faces so dark you couldn't see their button eyes and the tops of their heads were crowned with white curly fleece that spilled onto their black faces. Their bodies were white with black knees. I watched them explore their new pasture with the baby lambs running and jumping only to rush back to their mamas. I had to admit the little flock looked awfully thin. "Okay, maybe these can stay until Ulysses Grant's estate gets settled." I pointed a finger at Esau. "But I'm not paying one red cent toward vet bills for these animals."

"We'll see."

"Esau, I mean it."

Esau's response was to open another section of the trailer and let out five Rove goats with long, twisted horns. "These goats are originally from France. They like to eat scrub, so I'll put them in the back pasture where it's overgrown. They'll clean it up real good for you."

"Those horns look dangerous. I mean that one goat's horns look almost three feet long."

"These goats are very rare, except in a certain region of France. Almost endangered. Take good care of them."

"Esau, you are not listening to me." I was beyond frustration with this man.

Ignoring me again, Esau went into the trailer and brought out more animals. Next stepped out Scottish Highland cattle. With their shaggy orange coats, they looked bewildered as they came down the ramp. One small cow came over and sniffed my pockets. I scratched her forehead and gave her an apple I had in my pocket. She took the entire apple into her mouth and squirted apple juice on me. I laughed and pulled out another apple. "You like these? Here you go, then." I threw the apple into the pasture. "Go get it."

The cow following the movement of my arm tagged after the rest of her bovine buddies into the pasture searching for the apple.

Another truck hauling a huge trailer pulled up to the pasture next to where the sheep were ba ba baa-ing away before grazing the newly mowed field.

"What's this?" I asked.

"Now, Josiah, these three animals look fierce, but they are very placid."

"Oh, God, what have you brought?"

"Just wait." Esau helped his assistant open the trailer door and let down the ramp. The first animal to emerge was a female white Texas Longhorn. "This is Tex's breeding mate. I'm gonna give him another day before I reintroduce them. She will help keep him calm." Esau slapped her rump and she loped into the pasture.

Next shambled out the largest bull I had ever seen. I think I gasped. I know I stepped back in fear.

"This is a Belgian Blue bull. He's very sweet, Josiah. Don't be frightened."

"You can't possibly be thinking of leaving this hunk of oversized meat with me. This bull is lots bigger than Tex, and Tex is huge. This Belgian Blue must weigh close to three thousand pounds!"

The assistant grabbed the halter on the bull's face and led him into the pasture.

Esau said, "See, I told you he was gentle."

A mottled blue-gray Belgian Blue cow with a calf shambled out of the trailer, following the bull.

"What's that scar on her side?" I asked, referring to the cow.

25

"Sometimes the cows have to have a cesarean for birthing as the breed is double-muscled, and the birth canals are sometimes too small for the calves."

"And you don't see a problem with breeding bulls with females, which are too small to deliver their babies?"

"I see a great many things wrong with our attitudes toward animals. I do what I can when I can, but one thing I can't do is change the world. Please, Josiah, help me out with these animals."

"You owe me one, Esau. I mean *really* owe me. I just know I'm going to regret this."

Esau smiled, saying, "You're a peach. My assistant will water and feed them for today. I want to check on Tex now."

"Can't they just munch on grass?" I asked, following Esau.

"They need supplements to regain their weight and health."

I walked with Esau to the stable where we found Tex munching quietly on hay and sweet feed. He glanced disdainfully at us with one of his long horns clicking a side of the stall before returning to his feed.

Esau observed through the wire stall door. "He looks much improved. How's his behavior?"

"So far so good. I need to change his bedding, but I'm afraid to open the stall door."

"I see you have a door on the backside of the stall."

"It leads to a dry paddock."

"Put a roll of hay in the paddock in there with him. If he does okay, we can move him into a grass pasture."

"I hope 'we' means 'you.' Bring some sedatives with you just in case. I can already tell that he is getting restless. I am feeding Tex constantly to keep him happy."

"He does need to gain weight, but too much food might disrupt his digestive system."

Irritated at Esau's complaint, I insisted, "Then take the eating machine with you."

Esau ignored me and went about his business.

Angry, I went about mine. I felt like venting so I went over to Lady Elsmere's home. Everyone calls it the Big House. It is a white, antebellum mansion, which my late husband restored when Her Ladyship came back from England after her second husband died. Lady Elsmere was a shriveled, old lady who loved expensive jewelry, gossip, bourbon neat, and me. Thank goodness she was fond of me because Lady Elsmere, aka June Webster from Monkey's Eyebrow, Kentucky wielded much power in the Bluegrass area. I would hate to be on her bad side. Many had discovered it was not a comfortable place to be.

I entered the Big House through the kitchen and met Bess, the chef. "They are in Lady Elsmere's bedroom. I hope you are here to collect that dog of yours," she spat out.

I teased, "You sound cranky, Bess. Knee bothering you again?"

Bess threw a dab of flour at me.

I had left Baby at the Big House until I could sort out this mess with Esau. I was afraid the dog might get hurt. "Was Baby bad?"

"Not really. Just slobbery and stinky."

"He does not stink, Bess. He gets regular baths. You just don't like him."

"I don't like that slobber puss drooling all over my kitchen. Now take him home."

I had to confess that Baby did salivate a prolific amount of gooey, nasty strings of thick mucus. It was a trait of the breed. Nothing I could do about it except follow him around with a towel and wipe his face occasionally, but English Mastiffs are unwaveringly loyal. No matter what danger, Baby was always by my side. Well, almost always.

Going upstairs in a rickety elevator, I found Her Ladyship's bedroom door open. I discovered Lady Elsmere in her wheelchair with Franklin, one of my good friends, and Baby huddled around a window with binoculars gawking at my property.

Let me correct that. Baby did not have binoculars, but had his massive paws on the sill with his head stretching out of the open window as he was gaping as well. As soon as he heard me, Baby jumped down, almost knocking Franklin out of the window in his effort to run to me. I was happy my dog was glad to see me. "Hey, Baby," I cooed as I scratched his ears.

"What the hell is that monster in your pasture? Looks like something Dr. Frankenstein would conjure up," Lady Elsmere said, swinging her wheelchair around to face me.

"Which one?" I asked, innocently, knowing which animal she was referring to.

"That blue-gray looking thing. Looks like it came from a horror show."

"Scary-looking, isn't he? He is a Belgian Blue, bred specifically for meat production." I grabbed Franklin's binoculars and sat on the window sill, peering out myself. Fortunately, the Belgian Blue bull was grazing along with the other three cows. He seemed content—for the moment.

"Those fences are not going to hold those Long-horns and Belgian Blues if they decide to make a run for it. I can't have them coming over here and hurting my Thoroughbreds."

"Esau said he was looking for a place to put them."

"You know he's lying. Put those animals back where they came from."

"Esau said he can't and"—I slid on the floor in defeat—"Jumping Jehoshaphat, I've lost my train of thought. I don't know if I'm coming or going. My routine is a mess. That Longhorn is tearing my stable up. He gnaws on the wood, knocks over his water bucket all the time, and bellows constantly while shying at every noise. I could just cry."

Franklin, wearing one of Lady Elsmere's priceless tiaras, grabbed back his binoculars. Let me explain who Franklin Wickliffe is. He is the younger brother of the man I am dating—Hunter Wickliffe. Franklin is also the ex-boyfriend of Matthew Garth, who is my BFF. He is brash, fond of expensive jewelry, and loads of fun. I am generally very tender toward Franklin, but not at this particular moment.

"You must be entering menopause," Franklin commented, peering at my farm. "Poor girl." He turned and patted my arm.

"Your tiara is slipping, dear," I replied, giving Franklin the once-over. "What getup have you got on?" I pawed the purple taffeta evening dress he had put over his clothes. I turned to Lady Elsmere. "You're letting him go through your dresses now?"

Lady Elsmere shrugged and pushed Franklin away from the window with her bony hand, dripping with diamond bracelets.

"Well, excuse you," complained Franklin in a snit.

I protested, "Don't worry about me sitting on the floor in tears."

Ignoring me, Lady Elsmere looked through her binoculars and mused, "Oh, dear. What's Esau planning?"

I scooted closer to the window. "What's going on? Why did you say that?" Rising up on my knees, I huddled between Franklin and Lady Elsmere, looking out. I spied Esau take my new tractor and haul a roll of hay, depositing it in the dry paddock. Then he and his assistant wrenched open the double doors to Tex's stall. As soon as the doors were opened, they ran and leapt over the fences.

Nothing happened at first.

Slowly a snout appeared out the stall's back door. Then a face. Then a face with horns the length of a pickup truck bed. Then withers. Then the massive barrel-shaped body. Then finally the back end until the Texas Longhorn was entirely outside. He gazed about the paddock seemingly confused. That is until he spied the huge roll of hay—expensive hay intended for my boarded horses I might add.

Tex ran toward the hay with his head lowered and butted against it. Reacting to the hay roll as an enemy, Tex took his horns and dismembered the one thousand pound roll with delightful abandonment until my nice clean hay lay in shreds on the paddock's dirt turf. Then Tex proceeded to stomp on the hay, urinate on it, and finally lay in it. He did everything but eat it, which is the hay's purpose.

"Tex is so ungrateful," I muttered.

"Is that the Kraken's name?" Franklin asked.

"Yes, and now I'm saddled with his girlfriend, too."

"How did this come about?" asked Lady Elsmere, whose first husband invented a doohickey which made them rich. While on vacation in Europe, he passed away. Then June had the good fortune to meet a very wealthy peer of the realm. The grieving widow entranced Lord Elsmere, who needed a public wife, but not a private female companion. You get my drift.

Lord Elsmere was fond of June Webster and proposed a deal to her. He would make June into a *Lady*, confer money and jewels on her, and spoil her rotten if she would not make waves about his personal life. This was at a time when a different sexual preference was socially and legally a taboo in England. Since June was ready for a new adventure, she accepted and the two spent many amicable years together until he too passed away. When that happened, June packed up her title, jewels, sterling reputation, lots and lots of greenbacks, and came home to Kentucky. The title and estate went to Lord Elsmere's nephew, Anthony. The less said about Anthony the better.

Let's get back to Lady Elsmere. I call her June in private, but Lady Elsmere in public. I need to tell you I love that shriveled-up old biddy. We've shared many a laugh, many a tear, and many a genteel cup of tea spiked with the most expensive bourbon known to man. Her Ladyship always has my back.

"I found Tex yesterday when he had busted into Comanche's pasture and was threatening him. Mike had to put several darts into him to calm the beast down."

Lady Elsmere waved her hand as though batting my face. "I know all that. Get on with the story. Whose bull? Where did he come from? How did he get here?"

"I'm trying to tell you if you would give me a chance."

"Yeah, June, you should know better than to interrupt Josiah," Franklin remarked, acerbically.

I narrowed my eyes and said, "Shut up, Franklin."

He stuck his tongue out at me.

"As I was saying—after Mike and his men got Tex into a stall, Esau came. He said he knew the owner of the bull. Tex is from an exotic breeding facility in Madison County."

"Tex swam the Kentucky River?" Franklin asked, incredulously.

"We think so. He must have found the low spot near our boats and come through the woods. He's all battered and bruised. Something spooked that bull to make him run."

June asked, "Is his owner Ulysses Grant?"

I looked at her surprised. "Yes, you know him?"

"Unfortunately. I was to be an investor in his breeding business, but when I saw how he treated his animals, I backed out."

"That explains a lot. Esau and I went to see Mr. Grant, and we found the main barn dirty and in shambles. So, this wasn't a one-time thing with the Longhorn?"

"There's a huge demand for exotic animals with big money involved. Besides, I wanted to keep these breeds alive and the genetic stock strong. The problem was Ulysses. He didn't provide a safe and healthy home for his animals. He was too rough and flaunted his dominance over them. When he didn't change after several of my complaints, I pulled my financing. I also complained to the authorities, but nothing was done. He was bringing significant money into the county. When that occurs, people tend to look the other way. My feeling is that one's relationship with an animal should be a partnership."

"When was this?"

"I'd say about twelve years ago." Lady Elsmere pulled a pack of cigarettes from a side pocket of her wheelchair, lit one, and blew the smoke out of the window. "How is Ulysses?"

"He's dead, June. I'm sorry."

Lady Elsmere became silent for a moment before speaking. "How?"

"Looks like Tex might have done it."

She took another puff. "Doesn't surprise me. Sooner or later, karma makes its move."

Franklin and I exchanged glances. We both believed Lady Elsmere's sentiment.

Sooner or later, karma does make its move—when one least expects it.

6

I checked on my boarded horses, which Esau had placed in safe keeping on Lady Elsmere's farm. That meant I would lose my boarding fees that month because I had to cover the cost of keeping them with June, but I had no choice. The bulls were too volatile to let the expensive racehorses stay on my property. I moved my pinto Morning Glory, llamas, sheep, and my personal rescue racehorses to the back of my farm. Unless the cattle escaped, Grant's animals would have no interactions with my critters. Esau just had to find the interlopers another home—and soon.

I was filling water tanks and feed containers for my horses at Lady Elsmere's stable when I heard someone approach. I don't like people sneaking up on me, so I quickly picked up a bedding rake and swung around.

Baby immediately got in front of me and growled.

"Whoa, there little lady. I mean no harm," the man said, throwing up his hands. The stranger smiled and held out a hand to Baby. "Here, buddy. Take a sniff.

I'm not a bad guy."

Baby stretched out his neck and smelled the man's hand. Sensing the man was not a threat, he butted the stranger's hand for a pet.

The man, dressed in a suit, gently scratched Baby behind the ears. "Good dog. Good dog." He looked up at me. "I've always liked English Mastiffs."

I was a little more cautious than Baby. After all, Ulysses Grant was killed in a barn. "Who are you? Don't you know better than to approach someone in a barn without calling out?"

He announced, "I'm Lucas McCain. I'm the homicide detective working on the Ulysses Grant case." He pulled his ID from a jacket pocket and showed it to me. "We met the other day."

Then I recognized the Tootsie Roll man and felt a little embarrassed swinging a metal rake at him, which I quickly put down. "I remember now. You were the detective who questioned us at Grant's barn. I'm sorry, but you startled me."

"Didn't mean to. My bad." McCain traced the scar alongside Baby's face. "What happened to the big fella's eye?"

"A cop shot him when he was a puppy."

"Oh."

"The cop's dead now, but then I suppose you already know that. You wouldn't have come out here unless you verified who I was. That's how cops work."

Raising an eyebrow, the man withdrew his hand. "You might say I did a little gumshoe work before I came out."

"I'm very busy, Detective. What can I do for you?" I pulled Baby away and made him sit.

"I want to take a look at that Texas Longhorn. I understand you have him."

"Was Mr. Grant impaled by the Longhorn?"

"We're still making that determination."

I gave the detective a queer look. "I think it would be obvious if Mr. Grant was gored. Was he or wasn't he?"

"He was gored."

"Was that the cause of the man's death?"

"Coroner still making a determination."

"So it is an undetermined death. Tex could have gored Grant after he was already dead or dying. Was the man gored from the front or the back?"

McCain shifted impatiently. "No comment. I would like to look at the bull. Also, the rest of Mr. Grant's animals were removed from the premises. Do you know where they are?"

"Esau Clay moved them because they were in bad shape. They needed care, so he brought them to me. I have them."

McCain raised his eyebrows in surprise. "That's theft, you know."

"As a licensed vet, Dr. Clay has the authority to

relocate the animals if he thinks harm will come to them at their original site. That's why he moved them. I'm just taking care of them for now. Once Grant's estate is settled, the new owner can come and get them and, I might add, make restitution for their care. I can't wait for them to be removed because they are costing me a small fortune in food."

"Don't they eat grass?"

"As well as supplements and special feed. One of the Valais Blacknose ewes is having trouble with her milk, so I have to bottle feed her lamb. Do you know how many times a day a lamb has to be fed?"

"Hmm." McCain rubbed his chin, not at all interested in my problems. "Can I see the Texas Longhorn?"

"You're not thinking of putting him down, are you? If he did gore Grant, I think the man had it coming. That bull was pretty beat up and starved. We are fattening him up."

"Who is 'we?'"

"The vet, Esau Clay, and I."

McCain sighed and repeated, "Mrs. Reynolds, you are not the only person very busy. May I see the Longhorn now?"

"Sure, give me a moment to take care of my horses, and I'll take you to him."

"Why are your horses on Lady Elsmere's property?" McCain asked, leaning down to pet Baby again.

"Because I don't trust those bulls. I caught Tex threatening Comanche. I can't have that, so I moved all the horses."

"Tex is his name? Sounds like he's dangerous."

"He was frightened and hungry. Animals get angry just like humans, Detective. Given the right circumstances, any human or animal can become dangerous."

"I won't disagree with you, Josiah."

"Please call me Mrs. Reynolds. I haven't given you permission to use my Christian name, Luke."

"Old school, huh?"

"No, just a person with manners."

"It's Detective Lucas McCain, by the way."

I left McCain standing while I filled up the water buckets and put sweet hay in the stalls while the expensive Thoroughbred horses were grazing in pastures far away from the bulls. Lady Elsmere's farmhands would clean out the stalls for me. We were bringing in the horses every night because a pack of coyotes had moved into the area. We also put my donkeys and goats in the pastures with the horses during the day. Donkeys are good guards against coyotes as they will chase the coyotes away.

McCain waited patiently while I worked, but he never offered to help. I thought that rude, but then again why should he? After fifteen minutes, I was finished and beckoned to him. We got into my little golf cart and sped off to my place. I wondered how he knew I was in one of Lady Elsmere's barns but didn't question him. The police have their ways.

I stopped by the dry paddock. "There he is in all his glory." We both stared at Tex who was bellowing and staring at the pasture that housed his lady love. Tex was chafing at his existence. He wanted to graze grass and be with his friend.

"What's he doing?"

"Calling to his girlfriend."

We got out and leaned against the fence watching the Longhorn.

McCain pulled out a pair of small binoculars from his jacket and studied the bull. "What conclusion did Dr. Clay come to about these animals?"

"They had been neglected. Tex, especially, seemed to bear the brunt of someone's irritation."

"How?" McCain lowered the binoculars and glanced at me.

"Esau will testify that the Longhorn was tormented. You can plainly see where he has been burned by a cattle prod."

"Isn't that how these bulls are controlled?"

"Only once in a great while would a person use a cattle prod. There's something else. I want you to look at Tex's shaft and testicles."

"No, thank you." McCain grimaced and tugged at his shirt collar.

"He's been harvested for his semen too often causing swelling and redness. I guess Grant had contracts for the sale of Tex's semen."

"Isn't that the purpose of a bull? To procreate?"

"How would you like someone yanking on you five times a day?"

McCain looked uncomfortable. I guess I was getting a little too personal.

"What about the other animals?"

"They are all underweight and neglected, but no sign of physical abuse. Lady Elsmere had business dealings with Ulysses Grant. You should talk to her. I never met the man."

"I did talk to Lady Elsmere. That's how I knew where you were."

Tired of bellowing, Tex spied us and slowly lumbered over.

McCain and I stepped away from the fence.

Tex stuck his wide nostrils between two of the fence planks and sniffed. Baby went up to him touching the bull's nose with his. The bull snorted and shifted his weight.

"This is the calmest I have seen this animal." I gingerly stepped forward and pulled out an apple from my pocket.

McCain grabbed my arm. "Is that safe?"

"I guess I'll find out." I stepped closer and held the apple so Tex could see it and then let him smell the fruit.

"Don't get so close," warned the detective.

"I think it's all right." I fed the apple to the bull like I would a horse with palm extended.

Tex engulfed the apple in one bite—his raspy tongue contacting with my gloved hand. He seemed to enjoy the apple and mooed for another. I always keep apples and peppermints in my pockets, so I gave another apple to him. Tex took the second apple and ambled away.

I said, "Well, I think he's relaxed enough for his lady love to visit."

McCain pulled out a list and visited the other animals in their pastures. What else did he have in those pockets? I was curious.

Following him, I noticed McCain was marking off the list after counting them.

"Are these all the animals from Mr. Grant's farm?"

"These are all the animals I was given by the vet."

"I talked to Esau Clay this morning. He said the animals he found were brought here."

I shrugged. "Then these are the animals found at the breeding farm. I never went to the pastures the day we found Grant. I stayed in the barn."

McCain twisted his lips.

"I take it that some animals are missing."

McCain didn't answer my question. "How rare are these animals?"

"I guess the Belgian Blues are the most expensive

animals here, especially the bull."

"He's that Goliath over there?" McCain pointed to the Blues grazing contently in their pasture.

"Yes, all three grayish-blue cattle are Belgian Blues. Looks like Grant was breeding this bull naturally. No artificial insemination."

"Why is that?"

"The calf is male. I suppose Grant was going to sell him when he matured. I think that with a *live cover*, bulls might be worth more. Would be lots of money for a breeding bull."

"What about the other animals?"

"Rare in the States, but common in Europe."

"They seem to be doing nicely, but they are awfully dirty."

I looked at the animals' matted fur and dirty hind ends. "I don't think they were ever groomed, but I'm happy with their progress. They've got a long way to go before they are in tip-top shape."

"Well, I can take Tex off your hands. I'll have someone pick him up tomorrow."

I suddenly felt chilled. "Not without Dr. Clay's permission, you won't."

"That beast is a suspect in a man's death. He needs to be examined by one of our forensic people. Testing for blood on his horns, hoofs, and face."

"We just got this animal calmed down. Taking Tex away right now will cause too much stress on him. I know you've got to do your job, but let's make it easier on Tex. I know a woman who can work with him while your people are taking your samples. You can do it right here. No mess. No fuss."

McCain considered my proposal. "What's this woman's name?"

I grinned. "Velvet Maddox!"

7

A day later, McCain was standing next to me in the aisle beside Tex's stall. Both ends of the barn were open and as it was a blustery day, the wind was kicking up dust in the barn. I put on a pair of safety glasses to protect my eyes. I handed a pair to McCain who waved them off.

"What's she doing?" McCain asked. We were both watching Velvet Maddox, an elderly, wizened woman with gray pigtails dressed in patched jeans, blue muslin shirt, and black ankle boots. Tex seemed transfixed with the woman scratching his muzzle.

I replied, "Miss Velvet is talking to Tex."

"I think this is dangerous."

"I gave Tex a sedative to take off the edge."

"How?"

"In a special mash I made with my honey. Tex is a sweet lover. Besides, Miss Velvet knows her way around animals. She's a whisperer. She could go into my bee hives without any protective clothing and not one bee would sting her. She's got a gift. She helped with my pinto, Morning Glory. Miss Velvet can read animals. You can trust her ability."

"How did she help you with your horse?"

"A woman fell under my horse cart at a parade. It looked like Morning Glory had trampled her, but Miss Velvet talked to my horse who saw someone push the woman. Turns out the daughter was behind the woman's murder."

McCain spun around to view my newly purchased farm. "Isn't that the lady's farm who was done in by her daughter? The girl was a chronic poisoner?"

"Yes, it is, and yes, she was. Her mother wasn't the only one she had done in. The daughter is in jail for life, so I bought the farm."

"Funny how that worked out for you." He paused as if thinking. "I remember the case. Made a big splash in the news. Yeah, funny how all these bodies are dropping like flies around you, and yet here you are with a new farm and equipment like that new tractor. Seems like you are living high on the hog."

I didn't like the implication in McCain's tone. You know how I don't like men talking down to me. "Look, I'm trying to help you. I'm trying to help these animals. I'm getting nothing out of it, but lots of bills which it seems I'm gonna be stuck with. You can take your snotty attitude and stick it where the sun don't shine."

McCain opened his mouth to respond but didn't get

a chance to as there was a loud rush of air escaping from Tex lowering himself onto the straw-covered floor while Velvet pulled down alfalfa cubes from his feed rack for him.

Tex munched contently on them.

Velvet came over to the half-opened, grilled stall door and beckoned to the forensic technician. "It's okay, honey. Tex says you can take your samples."

The tech gave one last beseeching glance at Lucas McCain, who motioned for her to go into the stall. "Can't we use a chute?" she pleaded.

"Don't have one," I replied.

"I'll stay with you. Don't worry, honey," Velvet reassured. "He won't bother you now. Explain to Tex what you need."

"You want me to tell a bull what I'm doing?" the tech asked, looking sideways at Tex.

Velvet nodded. "Like you would with a human patient. Remember—be gentle with him and no sudden movements."

"As if I'd be doing anything else," the tech murmured, stepping cautiously inside the stall. She carefully swabbed Tex's horns and snapped photos of his healing wounds while Tex grunted and slowly munched on his alfalfa. Velvet stayed in Tex's line of sight while the tech worked until she was done. Snapping her case shut, the tech was out of the stall lickety-split. She stopped by McCain and sputtered, "You owe me one, Lucas."

"See ya tonight," he replied. "And thanks." McCain watched the woman leave the barn and get into her van.

I got a sense that the two were more than work associates. "You dating her?" I asked.

"I'm married to the woman. There will be hell to pay tonight."

"You better bring home flowers and take her out to dinner."

"I think you might be right on that accord." McCain leaned on the stall half-door, staring at the Longhorn.

"Get up, Tex," Velvet ordered the bull. "Time to go back outside."

Tex rose and sauntered outside where he found his ladylove waiting for him. I had a farmhand sneak the cow inside the dry paddock while Velvet was working with the bull. He immediately trotted over to the cow. They sniffed each other, made some moo sounds, and then Tex tore up another hay roll while his love watched approvingly.

Velvet also approved. Dusting off her hands, she made her way over to us. "He's feeling much better. I think you will be able to move him to a grass pasture tomorrow."

"Well, this has been most entertaining," Detective McCain said. "Nice meeting you, Miss Velvet." He turned to leave.

"Don't you want to know what Tex divulged?" Velvet asked in a sharp tone.

McCain swung back around. His face looked less than enthusiastic. "Pray tell."

"Tex said that it was a bad day. Mr. Grant was in a fouler mood than usual. He kept hitting Tex for resisting, so Tex butted Grant with his head and knocked him down. Tex was in a rage and tore the barn up, but he didn't touch Grant again, who fled to his office."

"See there. You are telling me that this beast attacked Grant."

Velvet held up her hand. "Let me finish, Detective. Tex didn't like Grant, but he didn't hurt him. He eventually calmed down and broke into a feed locker, pulling out the feed and eating."

I said, "That's true. One of the storage lockers was open with sweet feed and supplement pellets everywhere. I remember the smell of molasses. If I could smell the molasses, I know Tex could. That's why he broke into the locker."

"What has molasses got to do with anything?" McCain asked.

"No one from your office informed Miss Velvet of the murder. Don't you understand? She's getting details of the murder scene correct because Tex is telling her."

"Perhaps, you slipped her a few details, Mrs. Reynolds."

"No, she didn't," said Velvet firmly. "Your office

called me and said that an animal needed a reading, asking me to come. I didn't even know it was a Longhorn bull until I got here. Nobody told me anything."

I pointed at Tex. "Don't you see Tex is telling Miss Velvet what he witnessed that day?"

"How is Tex communicating to you?" McCain asked of Velvet.

"He sends me mental images which I interpret."

Detective McCain scoffed, "I'm sorry. I'm leaving. This whole affair is ridiculous. I don't know how I got myself roped into this."

Velvet asked incredulously, "Don't you want to know what happened?"

"I know what happened. This animal killed Ulysses Grant."

"No, Tex didn't," Velvet snapped, "but he saw who did."

"Oh, for crying-out-loud," the detective said as his brow furrowed. "I'll bite. Who?"

"Tex says a man came in and pounded on the office door."

"This man came into the barn with Tex loose?"

"Tex was busy eating his ill-gotten goods inside the feed storage area, so the man didn't see him at first. This Grant came out of the office and the two men quarreled. The stranger took out a gun and shot Grant. He fell and crawled toward the office. The stranger heard Tex making noises and shot at him, panicking the bull and forcing him to run."

"The victim was gored. He wasn't shot."

"You weren't looking for bullet holes, were you? Go back and take another look," Velvet insisted.

"The coroner would have discovered bullet fragments."

"Maybe he wasn't looking for them or maybe the bullet went through Grant into a wall. Then the killer used something to poke a big hole in Grant to make it look like Tex had gored him."

Detective McCain glanced at his watch. "Thank you, ladies. I need to be going. Planet Earth is expecting me."

I shot a concerned look at Velvet following McCain to his car, relating more crime scene details. The detective didn't respond and drove off without looking at her.

Velvet wasn't happy. Standing with her hands on her hips, Velvet went over to the paddock, scrutinizing the two Longhorns grazing on what was left of the hay roll.

I stood beside her watching as well.

"Jo, you're going to have to hide those animals. If by chance, they find some blood on Tex's horns, they will put him down and close the case."

Putting a reassuring hand on Velvet's shoulder, I replied, "I know. I'll take care of it."

And I did.

8

Franklin and I were putting eggs from my heirloom hens into cartons when Shaneika walked in the Butter-fly. Shaneika Mary Todd is my criminal lawyer. You have no idea how many times this woman has gotten my fanny out of both the frying pan and the fire. Her mother, Eunice Todd, is my catering business partner.

The Todds are descendants of the Mary Todd Lincoln family, and Shaneika sits on the board of the Kentucky Mansions Preservation Foundation which oversees the Mary Todd Lincoln House Museum in Lexington. I have no idea where she got her endless supply of vintage couture suits and dresses. She won't tell me.

I looked up in surprise. "What are you doing here?"

Franklin exclaimed, "Not only that, but what have you done with yourself?"

We were both staring at Shaneika, who had shaved her hair, giving it a very close crop to the scalp. Wearing a black vintage Chanel two-piece suit with a white silk blouse and black pumps, Shaneika looked exactly like what she was—a stylish, successful professional.

"When did you shave your afro?" I asked.

"Two days ago. Got tired of taking care of it. Too much work. What do you think of my new hairdo?"

"The hair is a radical look for you, but I think the pearls are a bit too much with the Dwayne Johnson look," Franklin quipped. "However, the Chanel is divine. Haven't seen this suit before."

"I thought the afro made me look too much like Angela Davis. However, it did have its uses. Whenever I paid a visit to the district attorney's office, those young white lawyers would part like the red sea when they saw me coming."

"You look very nice, Shaneika. I've always liked this hairstyle on you. Shows off your high cheekbones." I kept putting eggs into the cartons to sell at the farmers' market. I was on a schedule, so I needed to finish. "I'm sure you didn't stop by to show off your new 'do.'"

"I came by to check on Comanche." Shaneika owns the Thoroughbred stallion, Comanche, which had confronted Tex.

"He's in the back pasture. Ornery as ever."

Comanche is Shaneika's pride and joy. He was a stakes winner and now, as a retired racehorse, stands at stud instead. Shaneika had bred him to Lady Elsmere's Jean Harlow and was expecting a foal any day now. I personally disliked the stallion, but I take good care of him.

Shaneika muttered, "Good. Good."

I studied Shaneika. "What is it? You look like you ate something that disagreed with you."

"I got this in the mail today." Shaneika pulled a letter from her briefcase and handed it to me.

Franklin and I read together until I pushed Franklin away.

"What?" he asked, edging toward me again.

"You're breathing on me."

"Who wouldn't be breathing hard reading that," Franklin replied. "You are being sued, Josey girl."

I threw the letter on the counter. "Who is Echo Trout? What a name. Who names their kid 'Echo Trout'? It sounds made up."

Franklin added, "I can't imagine the teasing at school with a moniker like that."

Shaneika grabbed the letter and put it back in her briefcase. "Josiah, you need to take this seriously. The man claims to be the nephew of Ulysses Grant and his heir. He claims that you stole valuable property from Mr. Grant's estate, and if you don't return those animals forthwith, he will have you arrested for grand larceny. Now the charge will be a felony since the animals collectively are worth over ten thousand dollars, although I think their real worth is more in the high five numbers. If convicted, it will mean significant jail time."

I was flabbergasted. "You don't take this seriously? Do you?"

"I do. Mr. Trout's lawyer is a pit bull. These types of cases are his specialty and the man always wins. We need to settle fast and out of court."

"Do I hear a little trepidation?" Franklin said, placing the cartons of eggs into a portable cooler.

Shaneika barked, "Put a sock in it, Franklin. This is important. Josiah could be in real trouble here."

I said, "I will be glad to hand over these animals as soon as Mr. Trout can prove these animals are his. You make sure Mr. Trout knows that I didn't take those animals. They were foisted upon me."

"Then Mr. Trout can pick them up?"

"As soon as he provides proof of ownership, settles the vet bills, repair bills to my property, feed costs, and loss of income. And make sure he realizes that if he sues me, I'll counter-sue him."

Shaneika snorted. "You are not being reasonable."

I looked suspiciously at Shaneika. "What are you not telling me?"

"Josiah, you don't understand. The animals were taken without permission, and you are housing them. That makes you an accessory. Dr. Clay is being sued as well. You will lose this case in court, and you may well be arrested for theft."

"Esau said no one was taking care of them. They were underfed and dehydrated. That's why he brought them to me."

"It doesn't matter. Mr. Trout is also suing you for

the estate's loss of income."

"What loss of income?"

"The sale of bull semen."

Franklin busted into a grin.

Shaneika warned Franklin, "Don't say a word. No quip. Nothing."

Franklin shrugged. "I can think of a dozen quips off hand. Real beauties."

I was astonished. "Where does Mr. Trout live?"

"In Florida, but he will be here in three days to collect the animals."

"Stall him."

"How?" Shaneika asked, looking back and forth between Franklin and me.

"Tell him the Office of the State Veterinarian is investigating the conditions at Grant's farm, and it needs to pass inspection first before the animals are returned."

"Are they?"

"They will as soon as you call them."

Shaneika chuckled. "I see. Okay, but you get those animals ready to go. Fatten them up and give them the last of their shots, but they are going with Mr. Trout when he comes. I'll notify you of his intent."

"I understand."

Shaneika entered the kitchen and took two egg cartons out of the cooler. She gave Franklin one last glance. "Nice costume, Frankie. You look like a sailor on a drunken three day pass."

I had to admit she was right. Franklin was wearing white bell-bottomed pants and an untucked, white shirt with a red kerchief tied about his neck. The only thing missing was a tilted sailor's cap. He looked like he was auditioning for a revival of *South Pacific*.

Franklin stuck his nose in the air and sniffed.

Knowing she had rankled him, Shaneika grinned and left, taking the eggs.

As soon as I heard Shaneika closing the front door, I turned to Franklin, who was nursing his wounded feelings. "Franklin, how would you like to do some sleuthing? I think something is afoot."

"My Watson to your Holmes? My Nora to your Nick Charles? My Paul Drake to your Perry Mason?"

"Yes. Yes. I get it. Well, do you?"

"Does the Pope live in Rome? Do birds fly south in the winter? Does a bear—?"

I cut Franklin off. "I get it."

"What do you want to do?"

"I want to see if I can find some bullet holes."

"Why?"

"Because I want to prove a murder was committed—murder by one human on another human."

"You know we'll get caught."

I boasted, "No, we won't."

But we did.

9

I ripped the black and yellow DO NOT ENTER tape off the door and pulled it open. I stepped inside with Franklin following behind me.

"Oh, it stinks in here," Franklin complained, holding his hand up to his nose.

"Looks like no one has mucked out the stalls yet and with the doors shut—just intensified the smells. Let's leave this door open and let it air out a bit."

"What if someone sees?"

"They'd have to be coming from the pastures since we came in the backside of the barn."

Franklin propped the door open with a cement block. "This place is creepy."

"Tell me about it." I turned on two flashlights and gave one to my sleuthing partner. "Follow me." I navigated a warren of bays and stalls finding my way back to the office.

"What was that?" Franklin asked upon hearing some squealing.

I made an icky face. "It may be rats. There was feed all over the floor when I was here last."

"Great. Just great. And I'm wearing slippers."

"Which do not go well with a sailor suit," I teased.

"I was aiming for comfort."

"I offered you some boots."

"Not those tugboats you possess. I have dainty feet."

We came upon the main corridor and sure enough we spotted gray blobs of fur scurrying away. Oh, gosh, I hate rats, but I had to admit they were doing a good job cleaning up the spilled feed on the concrete floor. That meant there would be lots of baby rats in the future for the barn. I shivered. *Get a grip, girl!*

"Ever see the movie *Willard*?"

"Really, Franklin. You have to bring that up?"

He shrugged. "Just saying."

We made our way to the main office. The door stood open. I couldn't help but notice circles marked in black magic marker with a hole in their middles looking like something had been pried out of the walls and door. "Well. Well. I was right after all.

"Why are you grinning?" Franklin asked.

"I just love saying 'I told you so.'"

"About what?"

We entered the office, and I sat in Grant's swivel chair, pulling out the drawers from the desk. "Looks like Detective McCain did search for bullets and found them. Dug the slugs from the walls."

Franklin didn't seem interested in that bit of news. He wanted to search and then get out. "What do you want me to do?"

"See if you can pry open the filing cabinet."

"And look for what?"

"A manifest of some sort on Tex. Perhaps a list of customers. A copy of Grant's will. Bank statements. Anything that might help."

"Okay, but this seems like a wild goose chase."

"Rummage around, Franklin. Does this place look like a going concern? I think Grant was laundering money and using this breeding facility as a front."

Suddenly, a man stepped into the doorway. "I think you may be right."

Startled, I threw a stapler at the man's head.

Franklin shrieked simultaneously and pushed the man down. We both jumped over the stranger and ran—that is until a police officer in uniform stopped us.

Franklin and I threw our hands up when the officer drew his gun. I cried out, "Don't shoot! Don't shoot! We're harmless!" I looked behind me. Who was the stranger we attacked?

The police officer handcuffed us and marched us back to the office where guess who was dusting himself off. The Tootsie Roll man—Lucas McCain! Oh, boy, Franklin and I were in serious trouble. Where was my get-out-of-jail free card?

"I hate you for this," Franklin whispered. "You're always pushing things too far."

I didn't blame Franklin for his ire at the moment. I deserved his condemnation.

Elated at catching us red-handed, Detective McCain sat in the swivel chair, put his elbows on the desk, and gave us the evil eye. Not really, but I could tell he was plenty mad. "Who's your buddy, Josiah?" No more pretense of being polite.

I was in the wrong and knew it, so I didn't object to him calling me by my first name. "This is my friend, Franklin Wickliffe. He came along to make sure I didn't get into trouble."

"Your wingman failed completely then. What you were doing is called 'trespassing', 'breaking and entering', and 'tampering with evidence.' I'm going to overlook assault of a police officer with a stapler."

"Please take the handcuffs off Franklin. He's innocent."

"Implying that you're not."

"I'd like to explain, but first may I have a chair? I have a bad leg." I was beginning to wobble a bit.

McCain nodded to the officer blocking the door. The officer picked up an overturned chair and placed it behind me.

"What about me?" Franklin asked.

The officer grabbed Franklin by the scruff of his

sailor shirt and pulled him out of the office, closing the door.

"Sit down, Josiah."

I did.

"I'm all ears. Let's have it." The detective picked up a pencil and impatiently tapped its eraser on the desk.

I decided to take the offensive. "I see you followed my advice and looked for those bullets. How many did you find?"

McCain stared at me stone-faced and silent.

I tried again. "I can understand why you might be miffed that I broke the crime scene tape."

"Very." The angry homicide detective leaned forward in the swivel chair. "I called Detective Drake in Lexington about you. He said you were an obnoxious busybody who was forever in his hair."

"That's not very kind."

"He said you were constantly stumbling over dead bodies. Said you had a knack for it."

I said nothing as I couldn't disagree with what Drake said. I was always finding dead people. It was beginning to get on my nerves. Finding victims had begun with the discovery of Richard Pidgeon dead in my bee yard on my farm several years back. I've been finding corpses ever since.

"Drake also said you have a knack for solving the murders. He said he had never seen anything like it, but you have a nose like a bloodhound for sniffing out the truth. He paid you the compliment of figuring out the identity of the murderer long before he did on many an occasion. You have become a valuable resource for the police department—and him."

I was very surprised. "Detective Drake said all that? I don't believe it."

"Yep. That's why I'm not going to arrest you and your friend. You were right about the bullets. We found two in the walls."

"You're going to let us go?"

"After we have a little talk."

"Can you take off the handcuffs please? It's not like I can outrun you, and the feeling is going out of my hands."

"Sure, but no funny business." McCain got up and un-cuffed me.

"And my friend?"

McCain twisted his lips. I had noticed this was something he did when annoyed. "Sure." He opened the door and ordered the police officer to un-cuff Franklin, who was sitting on a hay bale. Then he slammed the office door shut again, going back to his chair. "Let's take it from the top. Why are you here?"

"I was worried that you were going to put Tex down regardless of what you found. I was looking for something to save him."

"I hardly think you are worried about that crazy bull after all the damage he did to your property."

"He's growing on me."

"What's the real reason and I want no *bull* from you."

I winced at the pun. "A man named Echo Trout is threatening to sue me if I don't give him back Mr. Grant's animals. He claims he is Grant's nephew and heir. I want recompense for rescuing those animals, but I'm very leery about handing these critters over to someone who is associated with Grant. You may not believe this, but I am concerned about their welfare. I don't like to see animals mishandled."

"In other words, you are trying to save your skin."

"I am trying to save everyone's skin. Hey, Detective, it doesn't take Sherlock Holmes to know that something fishy was going on here. Look at the state of the facility. If it was on the up and up, it would be spotless, the animals wouldn't have been undernourished and dehydrated, and golly, look at the condition of the pastures. They are in a terrible mess. I'm telling you that I don't think Grant was murdered over these animals. Something else was going on here, and I want to find out what."

I got a long hard stare from McCain. Screwing up my courage, I bargained, "Let's do a quid pro quo. I tell you things and you tell me things."

"That's not how I work."

"Bend a little. Remember Detective Drake said I was invaluable to solving murder cases." I batted my eyelashes at him.

Resigned, McCain sighed. "Mr. Trout is one of several relatives that are laying claim to Grant's estate."

"Laying claim? You mean old man Grant didn't leave a will?"

"Two relatives have provided us with documents but they state different beneficiaries and bequests. I reckon we are going to see more wills pop up in the future."

"So Echo Trout has no legitimate claim to his uncle's animals?"

"Not unless a judge says he does. We have searched the deceased's home and here. We found nothing of importance really. We even talked to his lawyer who claims Ulysses Grant never did a will through his office."

"Does this Echo Trout have a criminal record?"

"I think you would find his past interesting as well as some of the other relatives who have contacted our office. That's all I can tell you at the moment."

"Who are these relatives?"

Detective McCain stood. "You and your friend are free to leave, but don't come back. You interrupted a stakeout operation. You aren't the only one to think something fishy was going on here. We were thinking the same ourselves and were waiting for someone to rifle the office. We wanted to catch them in the act."

"That's why we didn't spot your vehicles. You hid

them. I feel like a boob." I really did feel foolish. How was I to know that this man and I were on the same page?

"I'm not even going to comment on that. Now I would recommend you take your little sailor boyfriend and get out of Dodge."

McCain didn't have to tell me twice. I immediately left the office, pulled Franklin up from the hay bale, and vamoosed like the wind. But not before we spied a green pickup truck parked on the ridge overlooking the farm.

Oh goodness, we really had blown the stakeout.

Sometimes I stink as a sleuth!

10

The next day was market day. I got into my booth spot and put up my jars of Clover honey and my rarest honey—Black Locust, which is made from the nectar of the Black Locust tree. The honey is almost clear like water and very sweet. Yes, there are different degrees of sweetness in honey as well as color and taste. It all depends on the nectar of the plant.

Pulling out my cash box, I put on my bee hat and settled in for the next six hours. Baby lay in his bed under the table. He's a fixture at the market and everyone knows him. He wouldn't take a snooze for long. As soon as a child approached or he saw a treat thrust under the tablecloth, Baby would make his way around and present himself. He loved the attention.

So Baby was ready. I was ready also and hoping to make a couple of thousand bucks today. I really needed the cash. Oh, I had money in the bank, but I hated to break into my principal. I was going to need that money for my health care when my body went south—

and it would eventually. My kidneys were acting up as a result of my fall down a cliff, but I don't want to talk about that now. Sooner or later I would not be able to work, but I would as long as I could and as much as I could. So here I was at the farmers' market on a chilly morning, standing behind my table, and waiting for my first customer of the day.

The market was already busy with regulars wanting the first pick of freshly-picked vegetables. I also saw people bringing their containers for refills on milk, eggs, and butter. A fiddler set up at the corner and was playing Bluegrass favorites—*Blue Moon Of Kentucky, Good Ole Mountain Dew, Foggy Mountain Breakdown, Rocky Top, Orange Blossom Special,* and *Rollin' In My Sweet Baby's Arms* to name a few. She always made a nice chunk of change at the market.

I already had several sales when the fiddler launched into *I'm Thinking Tonight Of My Blue Eyes.* I was tapping my foot to the tune when a woman approached and handed me a fifty dollar bill. "What may I get for you?" I asked as she stood staring at me.

"You can hand over my animals."

"Excuse me?"

"I'm Narcy Trout and I want my animals. They belong to me."

"Are you a relative of Ulysses Grant?"

"I'm his beneficiary and was told that you have my animals."

"I'd be happy to hand over the animals. Have you cleared it with the police and a judge? Your brother is also claiming the animals."

"I want my animals. They were promised to me."

"I hear you. I hear you, and I will only be too happy to turn the animals over to you as soon as I have proof of ownership and all their bills paid."

"Bills? What bills?

"Vet bills for one. The beasts were in bad condition which is why they were moved, but they are on the mend now." I expected Narcy Trout to thank me, but she stood motionless.

I noticed her bright red jogging outfit and vintage Saint Laurent purse, which looked legit. I pride myself on knowing designer bags. I have several myself from my younger days. They are currently collecting dust in my closet.

The woman stood blinking at me, her brassy blonde hair fluttering in the slight breeze. Her blue eyes seemed all irises and her lips quivered a bit. "I'm giving you one last chance to return my animals to me."

I repeated, "I'd be more than happy to when you show proof of ownership and pay my expenses."

By now, Baby was standing beside me and nudged my hand. He must have recognized the creeping anxiety in my voice. I don't want conflicts when I'm in public. Bad for business. I held the fifty dollar bill out to her.

Narcy Trout sneered while her thick features merged into a mask of hate. She picked up one of my Black Locust honey jars and dropped it, causing the glass to break.

I was so stunned I didn't react. I stood there with my mouth gaping open.

Trout picked up another glass jar and dropped it on the pavement, shattering the glass.

"What are you doing!" I cried, finally coming to my senses.

Snickering, Narcy snatched another jar and dropped it. By now customers had heard my cry and turned to watch.

I threw myself over my rows of honey jars, wanting to protect them when something hit the back of my head. I heard something of a roar, detected movement out of the corner of my eye, felt Baby pulling on my pants with his teeth, and someone pressing on the back of my head.

Everything was quite dull after that.

11

I woke up to a fabulous headache. Sitting in the corner of my emergency room cubicle was Matt Garth. He is my best friend and lives in a bungalow on my property.

We met at a party where he was engaged in a bet as to what Patricia Neal's character said to Gort, the robot, from *The Day The Earth Stood Still*. I knew the answer and whispered it into his ear—"Klaatu barada nikto." Matt won the bet and I won a new friend. We've been together ever since.

It didn't hurt that Matt is over six feet with curly raven hair and bright blue eyes that shine from a Roman patrician face. He is gorgeous and looks like the 1940s matinee idol Victor Mature, who was known for his wit. When declined for membership at a country club on the basis of being an actor, Mature quipped, "I'm no actor. Haven't they seen my movies?"

My heart never fails to skip a beat when I see Matt walking toward me. I don't know if I'm *in love* with

Matt, but I sure am *in lust* with him, but he is twenty years younger and a hound dog. You can't trust Matt with either men or women, although he has slowed his sexual escapades, since he fathered a baby girl. I can say with all honesty that Matt is a devoted father and a great friend. He is also an honest tax attorney. Yet, in the affairs of the heart, don't turn your back on him. Look what he did to Franklin. They were an item until Matt dumped Franklin for the baby's mother. They seemed to have repaired the damaged relationship somewhat, but it remains fragile in the best of times.

"Well, finally," he said, giving me a worried grin.

I lifted myself up on my elbows and glanced about the hospital cubicle. "How long have I been here?"

"About a couple of hours or more. You've been in and out ever since they brought you in. Got a nasty bump on the head. How many fingers am I holding up?"

"Three. How did you get here?"

"They called me as an emergency contact." Matt looked at his watch. "I've been here about an hour. They should release you soon."

"Where is Emmeline?" That's Matt's daughter.

"I called Franklin and he met me here. He's walking around with her. She started to get fussy."

I lay back down on the bed.

"Feeling woozy?"

"Just a little," I replied. "What happened?"

"Apparently a woman by the name of Narcy Trout hit you over the head with one of your honey jars. Don't you remember?"

I shook my head, which was the wrong thing to do. It hurt. "I don't remember anything about the incident."

Matt uncrossed his legs and leaned forward. "Do you remember going to the market?"

I thought carefully. "Yes, I remember setting up and waiting on a few customers, but I don't remember the lady in question."

"Just as well for now. It will all come back to you later after you've rested."

I shot up from the bed. "BABY! Where is Baby?"

"Detective Kelly took him to Lady Elsmere's home, and they are looking after him."

I lay down again as my head was swimming.

I heard the curtain swoosh and recognized Franklin's voice. "Is she dead yet?"

"I'm not dead, Franklin," I mumbled.

"Pity," he replied. Now Franklin and Matt used to be a hot item until Matt decided to marry Meriah Caldwell, the famous mystery writer. Remember what I said about Matt being a hound dog? Anyway, the marriage did not take place, but Meriah was pregnant at the time and Matt took full custody of the baby—thus Emmeline Louise Rose Garth. Louise is my middle name.

The dark curly-haired baby leaned out of Franklin's arms reaching for me and fussing when I did not pick her up. I was in no state to hold Emmeline.

Matt, fearing an explosion of baby tears, said, "Franklin, can you take her for a spin around the block again? I want to get Josiah ready to take home. The doctor should be here any moment to sign her out."

"Sure. Hope you feel better soon, Josiah." He shot Matt a parting glance before departing with the tired baby.

Catching Franklin's glance, I asked Matt, "What is it that you are not telling me?"

"A man named Echo Trout showed up at your farm with trailers for those rescue animals. I had to call the police, and there was an awful row. He finally left, but he'll be back. I'm sure of it. The man seemed un-hinged."

"Sounds like a coordinated attack. Get me out of the way at the market via this Narcy Trout woman, and Echo Trout comes to take the animals."

Matt said, "Trout was trying to ram through the security gate. I guess he didn't know that I lived on the property and would hear him."

"They sound very determined."

Matt asked, "Are they married?"

"I don't know," I answered. "I can't think of any-thing with this headache. Never heard of the Trouts until a couple of days ago. Echo Trout is threatening to sue me. Why all this fuss? It would seem to be less trouble just to let a judge decide who gets what."

Matt reached over and grabbed my hand, giving me a sympathetic pat. "The problem is that they will try again, and we now know they will use violence to get those animals back. I mean, who hits someone on the head with a glass jar in public? Obviously, someone without impulse control." He said as an afterthought, "Oh, by the way, you have honey still in your hair, but the doc picked out all the glass."

"That's why I feel so sticky." I felt my head. There was a bandage and lots of gooey hair. "Stitches?"

"Four."

"That many, huh."

Matt took a deep breath. "Josiah, I'm taking Emmeline and staying with Franklin until this mess is sorted out. I can't allow my daughter near this. Between those dangerous bulls and now the Trouts, I've got to get her away from the farm. I hope you understand."

My heart sank, but I replied, "I would expect a father to do no less for his child. You do what you have to do, Matt. I'll keep an eye on your place and collect your mail." I squeezed his hand. "It's okay. I'll be fine."

Matt didn't seem so sure, but I thought he was making the right decision. After all, people get hurt hanging around me.

"Where's this Narcy Trout now?" I asked.

"She's in jail until Monday when the judge can see her, so you have some time to return those animals."

"I'm not giving them up, Matt. This tells me those critters would be in bad hands if I surrendered them to the Trouts. They may be a pain in my fanny, but the animals have done nothing to warrant being mistreated. Ever since Tex calmed down, he's been gentle except for tearing up a hay roll or two."

"Suit yourself. You are way too stubborn as always, but be careful, Josiah. The Trouts are not playing. Echo Trout seemed unhinged, and we know this Narcy Trout is violent." He gave a heavy sigh and stood. "I'll tell Franklin to take Emmeline to his apartment. I'll meet them there after I get you settled at the Big House. Lady Elsmere is expecting you."

"Don't worry, Matt. It will be okay. I will be okay."

Matt didn't look convinced, but he went in search of my doctor.

I lay my sticky head down and wondered what I had gotten myself into. What had I said before?

No good deed goes unpunished!

Didn't I say that?

12

I stayed with Lady Elsmere at the Big House on Saturday night and all day Sunday where a hired nurse looked after me. Talk about being spoiled—the nurse even rubbed my aching feet. I hated to see her leave Monday morning.

After getting the green light to return to work from my regular doctor, I met with Shaneika on Monday afternoon. I was leaning on the fence watching Tex and his girlfriend when Shaneika pulled up in her Mercedes.

"Your security gate is bent. Looks like it really took a beating. It barely squeaked open when I put in the code," Shaneika commented, getting out of her car.

"Echo Trout did that on Saturday trying to get into the farm. Matt was here and stopped him. I figure Trout was going to ram that gate until he got in. Luckily it held, but it can't take too much more punishment. I'll have it replaced. Add that on to the list of bills for Ulysses Grant's beneficiaries."

"Yeah, Matt called and told me about it. I went to

ABIGAIL KEAM

the police department and got a copy of the report." She followed my gaze toward the Longhorns. "You've moved the bull out of the stable. What does that mean for Comanche?"

"The Longhorns were ready for grazing, but I'm keeping Comanche in the back field until his seeded pasture at Lady Elsmere's is ready. The grass has only started to grow. Don't worry. I'm keeping Tex and Comanche far apart. I know those two don't get along."

Shaneika studied the Texas Longhorns. "They don't look very frightening."

"No, nothing like I thought when I first saw them. Watch this." I pulled a couple of apples out of my pocket and held them up. "Hey, Tex. I've got a treat for you."

Tex looked up at the sound of his name. Seeing the apples, he slowly wandered over, moving his bulk gracefully until he pushed his snout through the space between fence planks.

Frightened, Shaneika stepped back. "Is this a good idea?"

"No sudden moves, Shaneika." I gave Tex an apple and one to his lady love who had followed him over. They munched quite contently.

I held up my hands. "That's all. No more."

As if understanding me, the two Longhorns snorted their disappointment and went back to grazing grass, but stayed close to the fence—just in case I pulled another apple out of my pocket.

I turned to look at Shaneika who had now joined Baby standing about ten feet away.

Shaneika said, "I take it that Baby doesn't cotton to the Longhorns. I feel his distrust."

"Baby is right to be cautious. Tex doesn't like Baby, but I can't blame him. Baby was nipping at Tex's heels the other day and got kicked for his trouble. Tex is all about self-preservation, and he's not about to let a dog dominate him."

Shaneika petted my drooling Mastiff. "Was Baby hurt?"

"Just his pride. He hasn't bothered the Longhorns since."

Shaneika did not seem excited about my enthusiasm for the Longhorns, but then I couldn't stand Comanche and she adores him. Different strokes for different folks. "Get in my car. I want to speak with you."

I suggested, "Why not come to the Butterfly? I'll make us a glass of iced tea."

"Mike is sending some hands over to fetch Comanche. He has a breeding session in an hour at Lady Elsmere's. I want to be there as a witness. Make sure everything goes right. The mare is top-of-the-line. I'm hoping for a first-rate foal."

That meant a chunk of change for Shaneika, so I obliged. Racing Thoroughbreds cost a lot of money, but breeding stallions is where the owners make their money back. For example—if Comanche's sire with Lady Elsmere's Jean Harlow proved to be a winner at the tracks, then Shaneika could demand a higher stud fee for her stallion.

I obliged and we got into the Mercedes. I drank in the aroma of her new car smell—you know that fresh scent a new car has. Shaneika's practice must be making good money, because she was close to being broke a couple of years ago. But then again, I give her a lot of business. "What is it?"

"Narcy Trout was seen by a judge. She is charged with 'public disturbance' and 'second-degree aggravated assault'. Unless she cops a plea deal, Trout might be convicted and serve five to ten years."

"Why not first degree aggravated assault?"

"Trout didn't bring a weapon with her. She was charged with second degree as the attending officer thought she could have killed you with the glass honey jar. Otherwise, it might have been a lesser charge."

"Is Narcy Trout the wife of Echo?"

"They are siblings. Their mother was Ulysses Grant's sister. Echo lives in Florida, but Narcy lives in Madison County." Shaneika coughed into her elbow and scratched her cheek lightly before turning to me. "Sorry. I think I'm getting a cold." She searched her purse for a handkerchief. "I was wondering about the Trouts' first names—Echo and Narcy. I checked

Narcy's records and that is a nickname. Her name is Narcisse Trout. Narcisse is the feminine form of Narcissus. Get it?"

"I do. So what? Their parents had a penchant for Greek and Roman mythology."

Echo was a nymph who fell in love with Narcissus, a beautiful youth. He rejected Echo's passion only to fall in love with his reflection in a pool of water. Unable to tear himself away from his own likeness, Narcissus wasted away until he died. That's how we get the word *narcissistic*. Narcissism is considered a serious mental health issue. My advice—stay out of a narcissist's way if you can.

"Don't you see, Jo? The genders are switched. Echo got the nymph's name and Narcy got the boy's name."

"Other than the fact that the parents had a weird sense of humor, no, I don't."

"I think there's something to it. I think it should be checked out."

I wanted to get back on track. "What is going on with those two?"

"It's not good, Josiah."

I suddenly felt alarmed. "Just tell me. Please." I knew Shaneika was procrastinating. "Just spit it out."

"Narcy Trout made bail. She's free."

My stomach lurched. "Well, that's just great. What else?"

"I talked to Echo Trout's lawyer and tried to make a

deal. He said the State Veterinarian contacted him about a complaint and is going to do an investigation at Grant's farm. Until then, the animals have to stay where they are."

"That sounds pretty good."

"Trout's lawyer said it didn't matter what conclusion the State Veterinarian determined as the animals were not going back to the breeding farm. Trout is selling them. It's the farm that is under investigation since Ulysses Grant is dead—not the beneficiaries."

"The State Veterinarian can come here and see the condition of the animals. I took pictures the day they arrived showing their poor condition, and Esau Clay can testify what shape they were in."

"Doesn't matter. The State Veterinarian has no authority to confiscate the animals or determine their future care. If neglect is discovered, the State Vet turns the case over to the local authorities. The problem is that these are farm animals which have less protection under the law than companion animals. You're not going to get much assistance from the authorities."

"Why is that?"

"Factory farms put the kibosh on added protection for farm animals. Do you really want to know how a chicken was slaughtered so you can buy it at the grocery store? If you did, you couldn't stomach to eat it. The slaughtering process of animals for our table is brutal."

"These are breeding animals, though."

"Doesn't matter."

"Is Echo Trout the beneficiary of Ulysses Grant?"

"His lawyer said he had a handwritten will. However, there are other family members contesting. It might take some time for Trout to wind his way through the courts, I think the fact that Narcy Trout thumped you on the head, and Echo Trout tried to ram his way onto your farm, shows that these two will do what it takes to get those animals. They are not going to wait for a judge's approval."

"The question is why. These animals are expensive, but not enough to risk going to jail over."

Shaneika said, "It's a puzzle for sure."

"Did Trout's lawyer explain why they so desperately want these animals?"

"I asked, but he wouldn't say. I don't think he knew."

"Now what?"

"My advice is to give the animals to Echo Trout. I don't think the Trouts are going to stop harassing you. Trout has an arrest record for domestic violence and we've seen what his sister can do when provoked. Otherwise, you're putting yourself in more danger. Who knows what these animals can cost you, and I don't mean just in upkeep?" She jabbed her finger in my face. "You know that domestic violence and animal abuse are companion behaviors. Don't be a fool,

Josiah. The Trouts are dangerous."

I slumped back in the Mercedes' luxurious, heated seat. I knew the right thing to do was protect those animals, but I had been thrown off a cliff, shot at, had my friends shot, my house set on fire, my own animals mistreated by miscreants who wanted to force my hand. Now I've been attacked with my own glass jar of honey and my front security gate rammed. I looked outside the car window at Baby who was waiting patiently for me. The scars on his face cut me to the quick causing tears to spill over and run down my face. How many more friends would pay for my stubbornness?

Even Matt and Franklin knew it was time to throw in the towel and stay away until this mess was settled. I don't blame them at all.

There were two *right* things to do—one for Ulysses Grant's animals and another for my friends and myself. If I chose one way, the others would suffer. I had some hard thinking before me.

I would have to pray on it.

13

I didn't do much work for the next several days. I went to my regular doctor for another checkup. He said I was healing nicely. He also took a sample of my urine for tests. Said he would get back to me. You know I've been having problems with my kidneys. Wish me luck there.

That afternoon was devoted to shearing. Once a year, I have a professional shearer come to the farm to shear my llama mama and baby, my rescue sheep and goats. She even gives Baby a nice clip for summer. I asked her if she would also shear Grant's animals.

"Which animals?" she asked, curiously while looking at her watch pinned to her shirt. She was on a tight schedule.

I pointed to the Valais Blacknose sheep. "There are also Rove goats in the back pasture."

The shearer studied the sheep. "I am familiar with these animals. Aren't they Ulysses Grant's?"

"You know him?"

"Yep, and I quit working for the man. It's been two years. In fact, after I finished my last job for him, I reported Grant to the county's animal shelter."

"What happened?"

"I don't know. No one ever contacted me again."

"Why did you quit?"

"I know healthy farm animals. I know what their fur and fleece should look like. I was finding massive infections of lice, worms, ticks—you name it in their fur. Now, I expect a dirty fleece. Sometimes matted and splattered with manure—that comes with the territory with pasture animals—but what I experienced was beyond the pale. I told him off before I left, too."

"What was his reaction?"

"He just shrugged it off. Said he was doing his best. He would hire someone else."

"Was his farm always in disarray? I found it un-kempt."

"No, it used to be first-rate, but then the man had a stroke and left much of the work to his son. The son moved and started his own business. He couldn't devote much time to the farm after that."

"What is the son's name and where does he live?" I wanted to talk to Grant's prodigy—badly.

"His name is Cary Grant. He lives in Richmond."

I chuckled. This family loved playing with names. For those who don't know, Cary Grant was one of the most famous film actors of the twentieth century. "Cary Grant?"

The shearer drew her eyebrows together before considering the name. "Yeah, must have been teased a lot in school." She paused for a moment. "Why do you want to talk with him?"

"I've got his animals. If he's Ulysses' son, then he must be the heir."

"Didn't you purchase them?"

"No. They were foisted upon me."

The shearer gave me a queer look.

"Ulysses Grant is dead. Didn't you know?"

The shearer looked stunned and made a silent O with her mouth.

I nodded in concurrence.

"You got Tex?" By the way, the shearer's name was Linda.

"Yeah, he's in the back pasture with his mate."

"He do that to you?" Linda asked, pointing at my bandage.

"No. Narcy Trout did that to me. You know her?"

Linda shook her head. "Never heard of her."

"She and her brother are trying to obtain these animals. Do you know Esau Clay?"

Linda wiped her forehead with the back of her left hand. "Good vet. Worked with him a couple of times." She bent over to gather a pair of shears from her equipment bag.

"He's the one who had the animals removed and brought to me."

87

Linda looked at me with new respect. "Whatcha gonna do with them?"

"I can't keep them, but I can help get them ready for adoption, maybe. I don't know what will become of them. I'd like to see them go to a forever home."

Linda grunted. "A shame really. Mr. Grant had very good bloodlines when it came to breeding stock."

"You mentioned Tex specifically. Had any dealings with him?"

"Only that the old man seemed fixated on him. Told me he was a dangerous animal and for me not to go near him."

"And?"

"The bull seemed pretty calm to me when Grant wasn't messing with him."

"In what way?"

"He was constantly harvesting Tex's semen for artificial insemination. He got complaints that Tex's sperm count was low. I think it was because he never let Tex rest—build his strength up—know what I mean." Linda winked at me.

"How do you know this?"

"I sheared in the barn close to the main office. While I was working, I overheard several telephone calls where Mr. Grant got chewed out. The customers yelled so loud on the phone that I could hear. They wanted their money refunded."

"You said this was several calls?"

"Yep," Linda answered, nodding her head.

"What happened then?"

"Mr. Grant hung up and then got Tex out of his stall and readied him for another sample."

"That's why you quit?"

"Like I told you, Mr. Grant had a stroke earlier that year, and things went downhill from there. He wasn't the man I had worked for when I first started."

"And that's why you quit?"

"Partly. I noticed that things were slipping from the previous year. I think he was having mental issues even then, but the last year the barn was in terrible condition."

"Such as?"

"The feed smelled rotten and the bedding in the stalls was old. I told you about the condition of the animals' fur and fleece, but when I noticed a red muscle car with a falcon on the hood parked by the barn was the last straw. I knew the driver. The car was owned by a well-known drug dealer about town. There was no mistaking it."

"If Grant had a stroke, maybe he was buying marijuana?" Since I had partaken in illegal drug dealing with my pain issues, I was a little more sympathetic than most, I guess, when it came to buying off the black market. Now don't get on my case about this. Kentucky has a draconian system when doling out pain medication now because of the over-prescribing of

Oxycontin in years past. The legislature basically threw the baby-out-with-the-bath-water. People, who are in dire pain, are told to use aspirin and such-like. Doctors are afraid to prescribe anything stronger, and patients suffer needlessly from chronic pain. Aspirin doesn't even make a dent for me on bad days. I need a strong pain medication—much, much fiercer than what is offered by doctors now. Okay, that's my little soap box speech today.

"This is a bad dude, Josiah. I'm not talking about recreational drugs. I'm talking about heroin, fentanyl, heavy-duty meth, angel dust—stuff that makes you crazy instead of giving a soft buzz or helping medically. You feel what I'm saying? I know several people whose lives have been ruined by this man."

"What was this man doing with Ulysses Grant?"

"When the drug dealer left, I asked him about the visit. Mr. Grant said it was none of my business. I said fine, but I was not going to work for a man who consorted with drug dealers. I got my pay for the job and left. I never spoke to Ulysses Grant again."

"What was the man's name?"

"James Ray Jones."

"Oh, a serial killer's name. Great."

"He's called Jimmy J."

I considered the name. Couldn't recollect James Ray Jones in my acquaintances, but was content that I now had two new leads.

Maybe one of them could throw a light on Ulysses' death?

It wouldn't hurt to talk with them, would it?

14

I discovered Cary Grant owned a heating and air-conditioning business, so I made an appointment and went there. I found a clean modern building with several workers loading heating units into a van stationed in an open work bay. The son of Ulysses Grant was giving paperwork to one of the workers. He wore khaki pants and blue cotton shirt with a patch that said Grant Heating and Air Conditioning. Like his father, Cary Grant was a large strapping man with huge, meaty hands, sandy, close-cropped hair, and expressive brown eyes.

"Mr. Grant?"

"Yes." He turned around giving me a big smile. He had lovely teeth, and I wondered if they were dentures as they were near perfect.

"I'm Josiah Reynolds. I made an appointment to discuss your father's animals."

"Is it that time already? Where did the day go?" He looked at his wristwatch. "Well, come in the office.

Let's get this over with."

I followed him into the reception room where several women worked. As I pursued Cary Grant to his office, a woman immediately rose from her desk and got us both a cup of coffee. I thanked her when she placed the cup on the side table next to my chair.

"Would you like a blueberry muffin?" she asked.

"No, thank you," I said, having spied a tray of doughnuts and muffins on a desk out front. They looked yummy but I was here on business—not to munch on delicious glazed donuts and bear claws—as much as I wanted to.

The woman glanced at her boss. "Just let me know if you need anything, Mr. Grant."

After noticing my non-response, he said, "Thank you, Janet. I think we are fine."

"Yes, thank you," I concurred, thanking her for the third time.

Janet quietly shut the door.

Carey Grant gave me full attention and asked, "What can I do you for, Mrs. Reynolds?"

"It's about your father's animals. I have them."

"So you confirmed in your phone call."

"I want to know what you plan to do with them. I have a list of their expenses thus far." I handed him an itemized statement.

"Whoowee! That amounts to a lot of heating units." He thrust the paper back to me. "What do you want me to do about it?"

"Aren't you Ulysses Grant's heir? These were your father's animals. Their expenses should come out of his estate."

"I don't understand why you have them anyway." Grant laid his thick palms on his desk. He didn't look or sound angry—just confused.

"Not by choice. Tex ran away from home and stumbled upon my farm, tearing up my horse barn and some of my fences."

"Tex was always a handful, but my father never managed him right. My father thought he could dominate Tex. A gentle hand should be used with him."

I didn't know if he was referring to Tex or his father. I took a chance. "Tex has calmed down since he's been staying with me."

"I don't understand how the rest of my father's breeding stock came to be with you."

"Esau Clay, your father's vet, went with me to notify your father that I had Tex. We found your father's body and the other animals in distress. Dr. Clay brought the rest of the animals to me for safekeeping until their permanent care could be decided."

"Mrs. Reynolds, I appreciate your dilemma, but I don't care about my dad's animals. You can keep them."

"But Mr. Grant, they belong to you."

"Your bill for their keep is more than they are currently worth. I'll gladly give them to you."

"I don't want them!"

"You took them. They are yours."

I was flustered and didn't know how to respond.

Cary Grant seemed sympathetic. "Look, I'm sorry about this situation. You seem like a nice lady who wants what's best for those animals, but I can't take care of them. Not the way they should be. I live in town and run a business. My father's farm is miles away from here. I couldn't visit them every day. Those animals need protection 24/7, just to keep them from being stolen for one thing."

"Your cousin, Echo Trout, tried to steal them. He says he has a handwritten will that states the animals and property are his."

"I know. We are going to court next month over it. My father would never have changed his will unless he was under duress. He hadn't spoken to either Narcy or Echo Trout in years. I'm sure he would have mentioned it to me if he had."

"The police think Echo Trout's document is authentic."

"I have my own expert who says it isn't. Besides I have a copy of my father's registered will, which was made with a lawyer since passed on. Maybe twenty years ago. I am my father's heir—not Echo Trout."

"Narcy Trout hit me over the head with a glass jar."

"Did she now?"

I bent my head over and showed him my stitches.

"She always was a hot head. Narcy is trouble. She's much more dangerous than Echo. You best be careful."

"Mr. Grant, can you tell me why the farm was in such disarray?"

"My father loved those animals. He did, indeed, but he had a stroke a while back and he changed. He always had a contentious relationship with Tex and took his frustrations out on the beast."

"That's a shame. Tex is a wonder to behold." I didn't mention that Lady Elsmere claimed that Ulysses Grant's behavior was somewhat sketchy years back.

"I tried changing my father's behavior." Cary Grant shook his head. "Finally, I had to let the hand play out as it was dealt."

"Couldn't you have declared your father incompetent and taken over as his guardian?"

"My lawyer looked into it, but Kentucky has very strict laws concerning guardianship of an adult. I had to prove my father was a danger to himself, and the proof wasn't there."

"You said you have a copy of the will? My attorney said nothing could be found."

"When Dad discovered that I was looking into declaring him unfit, he disowned me. I think I had two conversations with him since then. It's a shame it ended the way it did, but this is a sad story in many families when an older generation has declined mentally. It's worse than dealing with a willful teenager."

"Why doesn't your father's current lawyer have a copy of the original will?"

"Like I said, I have a copy of a will going back twenty years. Why my father's new lawyer doesn't have a record of it I can't fathom."

"What can you tell me about your cousins?"

"Bad side of the family. Their mother was my aunt. She ran wild as a teenager and wound up an alcoholic. Two kids and no husband to speak of—but lots of men in and out of her life. You see how it was. I warn you that my cousins have a reputation for being mean. My father and I had little to do with them. Oh, Dad tried to help my aunt when she was young and the babies were little, but nothing took. He gave up helping and wrote her off."

"What are their chances of succeeding with this handwritten paper?"

"My lawyer assures me that it will come to nothing."

"What are you going to do with the farm?"

"I am going to develop the land and live off the proceeds like a king. I might relocate to Arizona. I don't like winters in Kentucky. When that happens, I will pay for the damage Tex did to your property, but I'll not pay one red cent for anything else."

I felt defeated. One avenue for me to be rid of these

animals was cut off. I couldn't blame Cary Grant for feeling the way he did. He was not in the animal business and he was a city man.

I stood and held out my hand. "Thank you for your time, sir. I'll leave a copy of the damages with your secretary. Who knows?" I smiled brightly at him. "You might change your mind about them."

Cary shook my hand. "Mrs. Reynolds, there's not a chance in hell that I will change my mind."

I left the office discouraged, feeling quite sorry for myself. As I got into my VW van, I noticed a green truck parked in a side lot—similar to the green truck whose driver was watching the breeding compound when Franklin and I left the other day. Hmm. I thought about something else, too. Cary Grant had not asked one question about his father's death. He didn't ask how Esau and I found his father. What state the body was in? Did I think the bull had really gored his father to death? If it had been my father's death, I certainly would have been asking a lot of questions.

Lots and lots of questions.

15

My other lead was Jimmy J. Did I really want to speak with a strung-out, possibly dangerous drug dealer? I'm known for taking chances, but this was too much. Maybe I should just cool it and let the courts handle the matter? However, when I tried to let justice prevail in the past, I got in a jam and still paid the price. No. No. There is justice and then there is my justice.

I called Detective McCain and got his voicemail. Told him to call me back. Left the name of Jimmy J.

While I waited for his call, I bottled Clover honey, mowed a few pastures with my new tractor, paid bills, met with Eunice Todd about an event scheduled at the Butterfly, and had Lady Elsmere's men plant Glossy Abelia shrubbery in front of the fences aligning the public road. I didn't want to install concrete pillars, but I needed something to keep vehicles from going through the fences bordering the main road. Of course, it would take several years for the hedge to establish itself, but I felt better knowing that the plants would eventually grow into something that would buffer trespassers. Many horse farms in the Bluegrass use this type of shrub ever since horse rustling became prevalent in the 1970s. It's almost unheard of now to have a horse stolen—especially with hedges protecting the fences. Needless to say, I was busy.

Three days later, I got a call from Detective McCain. He was outside my property wanting to come in. I pushed the button that opened the main gate and met him at the front door of my house.

He got out of an unmarked, standard dark blue sedan that most detectives use in Kentucky and stood gaping at the Butterfly.

"What do you think?" I called out to the detective. This was his first glimpse of the Butterfly as I usually had met him at the stable. You can't see the house from there.

"I've seen pictures of this place in magazines, but seeing it in person is another thing."

"Come in. I'm making coffee and just about to take some cinnamon rolls out of the oven—if you're game."

"I could do with a snack. Missed lunch."

"I've got some tuna fish salad. Can make you a sandwich."

For the first time, the Tootsie Roll man looked kindly at me. "That sounds pretty good. My stomach is growling. Will you join me?"

I nodded. "I'll show you around." I led my visitor

through the foyer into the main living area.

He studied the cathedral ceilings, the mid-century furniture, the slate floor, the beige and gray stone walls, and the windows that blanketed the back walls which displayed a spectacular view of the Kentucky River and its cliffs. Several waterfalls splashed down ravines on the other side of the river from the recent rains.

"I see you like art."

"I used to be an art history professor. I very much like art, especially glass."

He walked over to several large Stephen Powell vases. "I recognize these vessels. Is that what you call them?"

"Vessel is a good word. Vase is another."

"The light from the windows really shows off these pieces," McCain said, admiring the three-foot-tall glass works.

"Go outside and look over the railing. I'll bring the tray out there."

"Okay." McCain went out the glass door leading to the patio and pool. The detective went to the edge of the cliff and admired the view, dipped his hand in the pool testing the water, and then sat at the patio table watching the birds eat from the feeders.

I carried a tray of coffee, cinnamon rolls, and two tuna salad sandwiches accompanied by dill pickle spears to the patio.

The homicide detective jumped up and opened the

door. "Here. Let me." He took the tray and set it down. After helping me put the food items on the table, he placed the tray by his chair. He must have been really hungry because he wolfed down his sandwich and then attacked the warm cinnamon rolls. "These are really good," he muttered, coming up for air.

"Thank you."

Wiping his mouth with a napkin, Lucas McCain took a deep breath. "Oh, that was good. Very good. I really needed something to eat. My sugar was getting low."

"My pleasure."

He glanced about the patio. "How does a person afford all this? Were you born rich, if you don't mind me asking?"

"I come from very modest means, but I was driven and so was my late husband. We made valuable connections while in college, which paid off in adulthood. My husband and some college friends started an architectural firm and did renovations of high-end homes. My husband renovated Lady Elsmere's home. But honestly, it was luck mostly—being in the right place at the right time, but we worked hard—very hard. Yet, I was on the verge of bankruptcy for many years after my husband died. It was a long haul to dig myself out of debt. When my husband passed away, the farm was paid for, luckily. Otherwise, I would have lost it and the Butterfly."

"A huge payout from the city didn't hurt."

"Oh, you mean the settlement from the city because a rogue cop threw me off a cliff and tried to kill my friend, Franklin, and my dog? I deserved every cent I got and I won't apologize for making the city pay through the nose for my injuries."

McCain sniffed and said, "Noted. Speaking of the dog, where is that big mutt?"

"Baby is probably over at Lady Elsmere's place begging for treats."

"She doesn't mind him coming over?"

"They're great buddies, and everyone who works there knows Baby. He'll be home when he gets tired. He might be in the barn visiting his cat friends. I call them the Kitty Kaboodle Gang. They're basically Baby's pets."

"Hmm. I'm surprised you give that dog such free rein. He doesn't bother the horses or Tex?"

I replied, "No, but he doesn't like Tex. Baby has learned to stay away from him."

"I see." McCain folded his napkin before taking a sip of his coffee. "Now tell me. How do you know about Jimmy J?" His tone was that of sudden irritation. Ah, my guest had gone from being an amenable lunch companion to a harried cop.

"I talked with someone who used to work for Ulysses Grant. She said Jimmy J was a visitor when she was there, and the two men seemed awfully friendly. When she asked about Jimmy J, Grant rebuffed her, so she quit since she knew of Jimmy J's reputation of selling hard drugs."

McCain asked, "Did she see Ulysses Grant buying drugs from Jimmy J?"

"No."

"Did your friend see evidence of any illegal drugs at all?"

I replied, "She didn't mention it, but why would Jimmy J be there if not for drugs? The facility is well out in the boondocks, and I doubt Jimmy J would be interested in breeding stock."

"Who's your friend? Want to give me a name?"

I ignored the question and proceeded, "And another thing, she overheard several customers give Grant a hard time on the phone because of Tex's low productivity. Wanted their money refunded."

"So the bull was spent that day. Means nothing."

I said, "Perhaps Tex is not up to par. There seemed to be a lot of fixation with this Longhorn. The Belgian Blue bull is worth three times Tex's worth, and now that bull has a calf which will grow up to be very valuable, but my friend says Grant was always concerned with Tex. Now why was that?"

The detective shrugged. "Who knows? The man had a stroke. People act a little funny after they've had a stroke."

"What if Jimmy J and Ulysses Grant were using the

breeding farm as a money laundering venture?" I suggested.

"Why do that? You saw the farm. It was rundown. If Grant was profiting from laundering, wouldn't he have used his cut to bring the farm up to snuff and purchase more breeding stock? I know for a fact that he had been selling livestock to make ends meet."

I shot back. "Have you checked bank records? Searched his house for cash?"

"Have you searched his house?" McCain asked me. "You seem to be all over this case."

Ignoring the detective's question, I posed another one of my own. We were going back and forth like a steel ball in a pinball machine. "What if Tex—how do I put this—was all show and no go?" I took one last bite of my cinnamon roll.

Leaning back in the deck chair, McCain said, "You think Ulysses Grant was killed because Tex was lacking in the "love" department? Some disgruntled customer killed him over that?"

Ignoring McCain's questions, I pushed, "Did you call clients who used Tex? Did you go through the purchase orders?"

"I can tell you with all honesty, there is no evidence for your theories. None. There is no evidence that Jimmy J was at the breeding facility in recent months and no evidence of angry, hostile clients."

I was crestfallen. "Really?"

"Really. You're throwing mud at the wall hoping to see what sticks." McCain took a sip of his drink.

"Did you look for a connection between Jimmy J and Echo Trout? They are about the same age. Maybe Echo Trout wanted the farm and hired Jimmy J to kill his uncle for him?" I kept pushing the issue.

Frustrated, the detective threw up his hands. "Stop, please. You are making my head spin." Picking up the tray, he loaded it with the dirty dishes.

I rushed to open the door for him.

The detective took the tray to the kitchen and gave the living room one last glance. "This is some house. If it was mine, I would never want to leave it."

I followed his gaze. "I guess that is a subtle hint."

"Cary Grant called me. Says you paid him a visit."

"I did," I confessed.

"Says if you bother him again, he's going to get a restraining order against you."

I related, "I was just notifying Cary Grant that I had his animals and asking for restitution from his father's estate. I did nothing to cause his wish for a restraining order. Seems a bit of an over-reaction."

"What makes you so sure the judge will rule in the son's favor?"

"He's Ulysses' only child. The law favors him."

McCain said, "Turns out the handwritten will that Echo Trout is going to produce in court was really written by Ulysses Grant. The handwriting expert the

Trouts used is a friend of mine and tipped me off. Now if you go around and blab your mouth about this, I'll deny it."

I can say that bit of news stunned me. "Doesn't a handwritten will still have to have two witnesses sign it?"

"Only if it was not totally written by the testator. Otherwise, it can be signed by the testator and dated. That's all Kentucky requires. A will does not have to be written by a lawyer."

"Cary Grant says he has a bona fide will," I said.

"Yes, he does say that."

"I suppose you asked Cary Grant where he was when his father was murdered."

Exasperated, McCain huffed, "Mrs. Reynolds. Josiah. Please stay out of my way and let me do my job."

"You were going to let the coroner rule Ulysses Grant's murder as accidental. You never noticed the bullet holes in the walls. I put you on to that."

"I admit I thought this was a case of animal aggression, but you're getting in the way now, and I'm starting to get peeved."

"Here's another tip for you. When Franklin and I left the breeding facility the other day, Cary Grant was watching from the ridge. I recognized his green pickup truck."

"That only proves my point. If you hadn't been there, we might have caught the son searching his father's place. Maybe for a second set of books, but we'll never know because you butted in. Did it ever occur to you that the son might be involved in his father's death?"

Ignoring McCain's outburst, I asked, "Doesn't it seem odd that people are interested in the old man's barn and not his house? Trout seems overly concerned about his uncle's animals but not his personal possessions. If I were you, I'd be searching the house for guns, hidden money, coins, bank statements—things like that. Ulysses was elderly, so he would have been old school. He would have more than likely left a paper trail and not used a computer. Did he have a computer in the house? I know he had one in his office but there was dust on the keyboard telling me that he didn't use it very often."

"This is exactly what I am talking about. We knew Cary Grant was casing his father's place. I wanted to see if he would go to the house or the barn, but you and your friend upset the apple cart. The man never made his move. You screwed things up for me. That's why I'm telling you to stop. You're a nice lady. I don't want to see you get into trouble. So I'm telling you for the last time, stick to your honeybees and rescue animals, because if you don't stop interfering with my investigation, I'm gonna arrest you. Understand?"

Undeterred, I mentioned, "It will be interesting to see how the judge rules, but I always say if passion and hate are ruled out for a murder, follow the money trail."

Detective McCain frowned. "Is that what you say?"

"Yes, it is. You should follow my advice. I have a nose for these things, but I will cool it, just as you asked."

He seemed relieved. "Thank you. I would appreciate your cooperation."

I said, "I'll see you out."

"Thanks again for lunch. It was nice to have a few peaceful moments in such a lovely place."

"It was no trouble." I walked him to the steel double front door.

"You'll stay away from this case? You promise."

"Scouts honor," I replied, opening the door.

"Good day, Mrs. Reynolds." Giving the Butterfly one last admiring glance, he turned and then left.

I watched the troubled detective drive away until out of sight and shut the front door.

Now you know I lied. Let's just call this a little fib.

I had no intention of letting this case slip away.

Yep, I'm a stinker.

16

I found it interesting that McCain didn't press me for the name of the person who had tipped me off to Jimmy J and client complaints about Tex's lack of performance. You would think a detective would follow such leads. Sometimes it is not what a person is asked, but what is not asked. That's when I knew something funny was going on with this investigation. I just didn't know what.

Whom could I solicit for information about McCain? I couldn't ask Detective Drake about him. He would inform McCain in a New York minute that I was snooping.

I would ask my pal, Detective Kelly. Yeah, that's what I would do. He wouldn't squeal on me, but first I had to find my dog. Baby had been gone a long time. I called the Big House and talked to Amelia, Lady Elsmere's nurse. She said Baby had left an hour ago and had headed toward the Butterfly. I thanked her and hung up the phone. Going outside, I called for Baby.

He usually came running after the second call, but nothing this time. I got in my golf cart and checked the Longhorns' paddock to see if Baby decided to have another go at Tex, but both bovines were leisurely munching on hay. I checked the other pastures but no Baby.

Perhaps he went to the barn to visit his cat friends—the Kitty Kaboodle Gang. Nothing. I checked every stall to see if he had fallen asleep in the straw bedding. Again nothing. I was starting to worry. I drove over to Lady Elsmere's place through the secret gate connecting our farms. It took me an hour to visit all the barns, pastures, and buildings on the huge estate. Everyone had seen Baby, given him a treat, and sent him packing. Baby had obviously made the rounds. I was taken that the farm hands, maintenance workers, and horse personnel were so kind to my big, slobbery Mastiff, but all said he had been heading toward home.

I ran into Mike outside the Thoroughbred breeding barn.

"What's the problem, Jo?" he asked, leaning against my golf cart.

"I can't find Baby. I've looked everywhere."

"Don't cry. Don't cry. We'll find him."

Was I crying? I touched my cheek and it was dry. Maybe I looked as though I was going to cry. I was worried. Baby was never gone this long.

Mike called security and told them to check Tates Creek Road.

"Oh, Lordy," I muttered to myself, lowering my head. I never thought to check the road. Baby never meanders in that direction. Still, could he have wandered onto the public road and gotten hit by a car?

Seeing the anguish on my face, Mike quickly said, "Now Josiah. That is just a precaution. We'll just make sure, okay? He could have been curious about the new hedge, and you know if any of our neighbors had seen Baby on the road, they would have brought him back."

"I understand. Thank you, Mike."

"While we inspect the road, why don't you go down to the river? Have you checked there?"

I shook my head, unable to speak. I was numb.

"Check the boats and I'll meet you here in twenty minutes."

Lady Elsmere and I keep our boats docked together. I have a little john boat and she has several luxury pleasure crafts. We keep our boat keys in a knothole in a sycamore tree. I hurried down the road to the river when I heard faint howling.

It could only be Baby. Was he hurt? Did Baby take a bad tumble? Had he been sprayed by a skunk?

I pushed the little cart as fast as it would go down the rutted gravel river road until I spied Baby tied to the sycamore tree. He was covered in blood. Stopping the cart, I jumped out and flew to my dog. "Baby. Baby. What happened?" Kneeling, I hugged Baby and searched for wounds. Then I realized that the blood was red paint! Jumping Jehoshaphat! What a dirty trick to pull.

Baby licked my face and seemed genuinely glad to see me, his tail wagging fiercely. I laughed with relief as I untied the rope from his neck. After taking pictures of Baby with my phone, I examined the rope. It was a plain ordinary rope that could be purchased in any store. I untied it from the tree and put it in my pocket. Then I searched the bank for footprints. Clean as a whistle. I stood quietly listening, hoping I could catch the sound of a motorboat, but all I heard were sounds of waterfalls on the opposite bank splashing downward to the green Kentucky River as it made its way toward the mighty Ohio River. I went back to the tree to search and found a note made from letters cut from a magazine in the knothole.

GIVE ME MINE OR NEXT TIME THE BLOOD WILL BE REAL!

It didn't take a rocket scientist to figure out who kidnapped Baby. I don't like it when someone threatens me. Threats really get my dander up, but I really don't like someone messing with those I love, and I love Baby! Deeply love that dog.

I guess this meant WAR!

17

The next day I showed the pictures to Detective Kelly. He seemed concerned going through them. Kelly and I go way back. He used to date my daughter, Asa, when they were in high school. He had been at my house most days for three years.

I saw him grow up and was sure the two would eventually get married—that is until Asa left for college without saying goodbye to him. Their relationship ended with a thud, but that's a story for another time.

"I don't think this guy is playing, Jo, and his sister sounds like a loony tune as well. I'd be very careful. Unfortunately, you can't prove Echo Trout kidnapped Baby. Why don't you have cameras down by the river?"

I shrugged. "Hardly anyone uses the river since the locks were closed. I hear a boat maybe once a month. No one had ever bothered our boats."

"Since you and Lady Elsmere share a dock, I would suggest a camera be posted there as soon as possible. I mean today."

"What can I do about this—legally? The man kidnapped my dog, poured red paint on him, and tied Baby to a tree after leaving a threatening note. Isn't that terroristic threatening?"

Kelly spread his palms out on the table. We were at Al's Bar on Lime and Sixth Street—Kelly's favorite haunt. "Nothing. You have no proof. Just suspicion."

A waitress came over and brought one cheeseburger platter, a bowl of vegetarian chili, and two iced teas. I asked for extra napkins and crackers.

"Can't the police department test for fingerprints?"

Kelly replied, "The police are not going to spend money on what they consider a civil issue. Since you recovered Baby, dognapping is not high on their radar, and you are in possession of Echo Trout's property."

"Maybe I have Echo Trout's property. That hasn't been decided in court yet."

"My advice is to give Trout those animals, so the man will be out of your hair." Kelly took a bite of his hamburger.

"That's what everyone keeps advising me, but I worry about their future. What will become of these creatures?"

Kelly looked down at his plate. "Josiah, I'm eating a cow now. We have to use animal protein to feed humans."

I nodded feebly. "I know."

"The one thing I advise you to do is not to confront

this Trout guy or his sister. They may be itching for a confrontation which they could use to their advantage. Promise me that you won't seek them out."

"What about their criminal records?" Notice that I didn't promise.

"I'm not allowed to search records on behalf of a private citizen. Only if it relates to a case that I'm working on. Sorry, but I can't help you there. Might lose my job if I did a secret search."

I asked, "How do companies do background checks on prospective employees?"

"You have to go to the police department and fill out a form, pay a small fee, and hope for the best. Why not do a Google search?"

"I did. Found some previous arrests for Echo Trout. Petty theft. A couple of public disturbances caused by drinking. Nothing on Narcy Trout except for some traffic tickets for speeding. She seems to have a heavy foot."

"There you go." Kelly greedily ate a French fry. "Want some? They are really good."

Shaking my head, I asked, "What about Lucas McCain?"

"Talked to a few fellows who had worked with him in the past. Solid detective, family man, and church goer. Not a brilliant detective but hardworking and steady—nothing untoward there."

"I gave that man leads, and he didn't bother to

make notes or pursue a line of questioning with me," I said, hotly.

"It could be that he had already talked to your sheep shearer friend about Jimmy J and didn't want to let on. You told me that you had already messed up his stakeout. He might be holding his cards close to his vest because he thinks you will get in his way."

"Speaking of Jimmy J, what about him?"

"He's a dude with a convoluted past. If it were my case, I would seriously be looking at a connection between Ulysses Grant and Jimmy." Kelly poured more ketchup on his fries.

"Any violence in his past?"

"Plenty. Like I said—he's a bad dude. If he did kill this Grant fellow, he might want to put the whammy on you because you are asking too many questions."

"Any connection between Jimmy J and the Trouts?"

"Again, it's not my case. I wouldn't know."

Frustrated I said, "I could just throttle Esau Clay for getting me involved in all of this."

Kelly advised, "It would seem to me the Texas Longhorn got you involved, and it snowballed from there. I would have a serious talk with Dr. Clay."

"Ever worked with him?" I asked.

"He works strictly with large farm animals and horses. Some years back, I crossed his path on a horse-napping case. He wouldn't remember me from Adam since I was a beat cop then."

I didn't know how to proceed. Looked like every avenue had been closed to me. "Kelly, is there anything the police can do?"

"Write a report at this juncture. That's about all."

I shot Kelly a serious look. "You know how quickly these things can go south. I'm not gonna hope for the best and believe that the law will protect me from harm. It didn't before. You say the law can't help me. Then I will help myself."

"I'm not being frivolous here, Josiah. I'm telling you what the law will and will not allow. You need to take heed."

"Then the law needs to be changed. It seems to favor the wrongdoer and not the innocent."

"We agreed as a nation that the accused are innocent until proven guilty. You haven't proven Echo Trout is behind Baby's kidnapping. Give me something I can hang my hat on regarding Echo Trout, and I will knock on the man's door."

I was angry, but I wasn't angry at Kelly. I was angry at the evil in the world. I was angry at the number of humans who cause such great harm to innocents. Most of us work, raise our kids, volunteer, try to be good members of society. And then there are those who will push and push until they get what they want. Echo Trout and his sister showed all the earmarks of sociopaths. I've dealt with these kinds of sick puppies before, and they don't stop.

I threw two twenty dollar bills on the table to pay for our meals.

Kelly looked up in surprise. "Don't be angry, Josiah."

"I'm not mad at you, sweet boy." I stood and kissed Kelly on the forehead. "You take care, Kelly."

"Where you going, Jo?"

"To buy ammunition for my guns." And with that announcement, I left my almost son-in-law sitting alone in a raggedy booth at Al's Bar.

18

Don't get your panties in a wad. I am frightened of guns. I have them but they are locked away. I'm not good with them. However, I was thinking that rock salt in someone's behind sounded like a good idea. How hard could it be shooting a shotgun? Just point and pull the trigger.

I was frustrated—that's all. I needed to be proactive. Baby and friends are my weak points. Franklin and Matt had already absconded to safer ground. Ticked them off my list. With Mike's help, I moved my rescue racehorses, mama llama and baby, my few sheep plus all of Ulysses Grant's animals before dark to Lady Elsmere's animal sanctuary down the road. The Trouts wouldn't know where to look as the animal refuge was kept a secret—Lady Elsmere didn't want people dropping off their unwanted pets on her. Since the animals were in pastures off the road, they couldn't be spotted either. I kept my peacocks and chickens. They were pretty wary of strangers, so I didn't worry about them.

Now for Baby. Detective Kelly took him. It was Kelly who saved Baby's life after the then puppy was shot by Fred O'Nan. Kelly was one of the first officers on the scene and discovered my dog injured in a closet. He also took care of Baby while I was recuperating in Key West from my fall. Needless to say, the two of them are pretty tight, and Baby enjoys playing with Kelly's children.

As for Lady Elsmere, no one would dare bother her. Besides, she sleeps with a loaded handgun under her pillow. Gives me the heebie-jeebies, but Lady Elsmere comes from a different era. Unlike me, she wouldn't hesitate to pull the trigger. She's a rascal, that old woman, and I adore her for it.

As I viewed my farm and home bereft of friends and animals, I felt depressed. Except for the wind rattling branches on the trees and the sound of squirrels chattering, the farm was quiet. No bleating from the sheep, barking from Baby, heehawing from the donkeys, snorting from the cattle—just an occasional cry from one of the peacocks, sounding like a woman screaming.

I hated the quiet as it was unnerving and unnatural. The farm looked deserted and empty. Even the Butterfly didn't elicit its usual glamour and cheerfulness as I walked into it. It was getting dark and I had just enough time to take a small nap.

I didn't think they would come before midnight.

19

Shaneika had called earlier in the day to tell me that the judge had awarded Cary Grant his father's estate, which left the Trouts' suit against me a big, fat nothing. The lawsuit would be thrown out.

The Trouts were left in the cold after Cary Grant's hired handwriting expert had testified that their will was suspect and wasn't dated properly. Why did Lucas McCain tell me that the Trouts' will was authentic? Was it to throw me off the track?

Either way, that meant if the Trouts still wanted their uncle's animals they would come tonight before Ulysses' son had a chance to move them. I trusted Echo Trout hadn't been informed of his cousin's desire to dump the animals with me, which meant Echo would come tonight. And hopefully, they believed Matt was still on the property.

I ate a light supper and took a nap. Around 9 p.m., my alarm went off. Didn't matter as I couldn't fall asleep any-oh-how. Too much adrenaline. I dressed in dark clothes, slipped into sturdy shoes, and loaded shells in my shotgun. Now don't judge me. I said I didn't like guns. Didn't promise I wouldn't use one.

I still have my old fashioned security monitors but now have a new system that alerts my new smart phone when the cameras detect movement. I had installed a new camera by the river road. I sat on my mid-century couch in the dark and waited and waited. The last time I glanced at the time it was 1:30 am. After that, I guess I fell asleep.

It wasn't until my phone began chirping in earnest that I awoke, groggy and confused. Then I sharpened up. I looked at the phone and pushed a few buttons.

Yep, I was right. Someone was sneaking up the river road. I would expect this person was to go to my front gate and push the switch to open it to let a trailer in. No noise. Quiet and efficient. If I had been asleep, I never would have known that someone was on my property.

Now why wouldn't they just climb the fences and push the gate open? I think it was because they would make noise fumbling for the switch and one of Lady Elsmere's guards would spot the beams from the intruder's flashlights. They still believed the river road had no security or cameras. I had fixed that after Baby had been taken.

I quietly opened my double steel front door to the Butterfly and sat in a chair on the portico waiting. I knew he or she had to pass by my house in order to get to the front gate. After five minutes, I saw a dark shape move across a field and climb a fence. Then I heard the crunch of someone walking on the gravel road. I still couldn't see who it was or whether it was a man or woman.

Didn't matter. I still had time. A screech owl called in the distance. A hoot owl answered her call and then a flapping of wings sounded.

The trespasser paused as if listening, too. Convinced that nothing was astir except for some owls, he started their path toward the gate again. It wouldn't be long before the intruder would pass Tex's pasture and see that the Longhorn was not in it, nor were other animals in their respective fields. It was time to act.

I stood up from my chair and raised my shotgun and squeezed the trigger. You might say I let the gun speak for me. It was loud.

20

As I told you before, I'm not very good with guns. The recoil almost knocked me on my fanny as the gun had quite a kick. Luckily, I didn't dislocate my shoulder and was so very glad I had shot at a dead tree in the opposite direction of the intruder. I just wanted to frighten the trespasser—not shoot anyone.

I issued an order to my phone and every light in the Butterfly, stable, equipment barn, Matt's house, bee yard, and pastures lit up like a Christmas tree. I could see Narcy Trout looking very stunned in the road until she came to her senses and ran like Old Scratch was after her—toward the main road where I'm sure her brother waited.

It would not do her any good as Mike was ready with Lady Elsmere's security boys. Four trucks poured out on the road from their hiding places and blocked a pickup with a trailer.

Spying her brother's pickup blocked in, Narcy turned and ran toward the river from whence she had come. I hopped in my golf cart and blocked the way, pointing the shotgun at her midriff. Now I had fired off both barrels and there were no shells in the shotgun, but she didn't know that. Seeing no way out, Miss Narcy stopped and held up her hands, but not before saying a few choice words. My goodness, she had a sailor's mouth.

It wasn't long before I heard the police sirens with their shrill cries careening around the crooked country road that led to my farm. Once they arrived, the police would take Narcy and Echo to jail.

I would get justice. My justice.

21

I was flabbergasted. The judge, presiding over the arraignment in Fayette County Circuit Court, threw out the charges against Echo Trout, saying there was no proof Echo Trout intended to crash my farm and steal livestock.

"What?" I muttered. "We caught Echo Trout red-handed."

"Hush," Shaneika whispered, sitting beside me at the back of the courtroom. The DA turned and gave us a blank stare, shrugging. He was as dumbfounded at the ruling as we were.

"But—?"

"Hush, I say."

"What does the judge think the cattle trailer was for?"

Shaneika pinched my arm. "If you don't be quiet, I'm leaving."

Mike, who was sitting across the aisle from us, had a bewildered expression on his face.

Then the judge gave Narcy a low bail figure, which was the same as no penalty at all and a distant court date.

Much to her credit, Narcy didn't gloat. She went with the bailiff peacefully after nodding to her brother who yelled, "I'll post the bail right now, Narcy. You'll be out in a couple of hours."

Great. Just great.

The judge dismissed the court for the noon lunch hour and quickly left for his chambers.

Disgusted, I stood and left swiftly as well. I did not want to run into Echo Trout in the courtroom or hallway, figuring he would no doubt come up to me and say something ill-advised, reveling in his triumph. If he did, there would be a fight as I would take the bait and lash out. My temper was up. Boy, was it up!

Shaneika and I made it to the parking lot before I turned and gave my lawyer a tongue lashing. "What in the blue blazes just happened in there?"

Shaneika replied, "The judge didn't feel there was enough evidence."

I widened my eyes and mugged, saying in an exaggerated voice, "Really? You think?"

"Again, the judge wasn't very sympathetic because the animals are not yours."

"That wet-behind-the-ears judge doesn't know the history of cattle and horse rustling in Kentucky. He doesn't know his peas from his mashed potatoes."

"It was a bad ruling, I admit," Shaneika offered, looking at her phone messages. "We still have Narcy's court date for her assault on you. She'll get some time for that plus we have a PPO against both Echo and Narcy."

"Why didn't the judge take the PPO for Echo Trout into account?"

"Because he wasn't on your property and wasn't within a hundred feet from you. How many times do I have to explain this to you?"

"It sucks."

"Yes, it does, but if you had warned me of this misadventure, I could have explained what was wrong with your plan. Echo can come after you for entrapment."

"How can I entrap someone who is already planning a crime?"

"Ask the U.S. Supreme Court about that. Now listen to me. Echo Trout is off the hook, but we have a real chance of convicting Narcy Trout on the assault charge if you just leave it alone. Stay away from her."

"She trespassed on my land. I didn't go seeking her. This is a load of . . ."

"Watch the language," Shaneika warned.

Mike came up to us and leaned against my van. "Well, that was a travesty of justice. Wait until I tell Her Ladyship."

"June probably knows already," I huffed. "She's got spies everywhere."

"Did that judge get his law degree on the internet?" Mike fumed.

I sighed and threw my purse into the van.

"The judge can only do what the law allows. They don't make the laws. That's the legislature's job," Shaneika mumbled, looking up from her phone. "Admit it, Josiah. You jumped the gun. If you had let Narcy open the front gate and then have Echo drive into your property, you would have had them."

"Once Narcy saw there were no animals in the pastures, she would have fled." Irritated, I grabbed Shaneika's phone. "Would you quit looking at that thing?"

Shaneika grabbed the phone back. "Keep your bad mood under control, redhead. I've got an appointment at my office. Need to go." She gave one last glance at her phone before waving goodbye. "Ta ta."

"Jo, I need to get back to the Big House. Can you drop me off?"

"Sure, Mike. Sorry I wrangled you into this and wasted your time."

"I do what Lady Elsmere tells me," he said, grinning. "She signs the checks."

Both Mike and I climbed into my antique but refitted VW van. I pulled up to the exit, paid my parking lot fee, and was about to pull out on Short Street when Echo Trout jumped in front of my vehicle. Trout did a little jig and made an obscene finger gesture before spotting a group of policemen walking out of the courthouse. Giving us one last sneer, Trout strolled away.

I muttered, "I wish that man would just fade away like the real Echo."

"That was Narcissus who died from gazing at his own reflection."

"I'm expressing my desire for that man to fade away. He's a big boil on my butt."

Mike patted my arm. "I'm afraid you haven't seen the last of that man, Jo. You need to be careful from now on. He looks like the type to rub salt into a wound and enjoy it."

I watched Echo saunter down the sidewalk, seemingly without a care in the world. I knew then the law would never protect me in this matter. I would have to be cleverer next time. That's all.

22

It was just a few days later when I got a registered letter in the post. It was from Echo Trout's lawyer stating that Echo Trout was suing me for disavowing him and Narcy of their constitutional rights. I was accused of causing false arrest and imprisonment, inflicting great emotional pain and suffering, and, last but not least, ruining their reputations in the community.

The lawsuit was a nuisance and would be thrown out of court like the last one. That's what I told myself briefly, but these siblings seemed to be coated with Teflon. All consequences of their actions appeared to slide off them like sunny-side-up eggs from the frying pan onto a plate. Maybe their lawsuit wouldn't be thrown out. Did I really want to go to court over this?

The entire mess involving those poor critters was costing me thousands of dollars along with my patience. I had better things to do than deal with Echo and Narcy Trout and the entire Grant family melodrama.

I went to Lady Elsmere's animal sanctuary where I had left all the animals, including my own. I didn't think it safe to relocate them back to my farm as of yet. It was relaxing to watch the animals graze and listen to the birds sing. I could feel my heart rate beat slower. I took several deep breaths and leaned against the fence.

Hearing a vehicle drive up, I glanced over to see Esau Clay get out of his small van. I turned back around, watching Tex and his girlfriend maneuver around my donkeys to graze.

"Thought I would find you here. You weren't at the Butterfly. Eunice let me in and thought you were over here." Eunice was my partner in our event and catering business. I rented out the Butterfly for special occasions like wedding receptions and whatnot. Eunice is also Shaneika's mother.

When I didn't reply, Esau asked, "Watcha doing?"

"What does it look like I'm doing, Esau?"

"Anyone tell you that you've got a nasty bite with your words, Josiah?"

"Frequently."

Esau put his elbows on the top of the fence plank and leaned, putting his weight on it. "Tex has gained weight."

"Yep."

"Looks content."

"He is as gentle as a lamb now that no one is beating him."

"Where's Baby?" Esau looked around for him.

"In a safe place."

"Oh."

"Oh is right. My entire life has been disrupted because of you, and then you disappear. I don't know how many calls I've put in to you."

"I'm here now."

"Big deal."

Esau's face brightened. "I bring some good news."

I turned toward Esau. "I could use some. What is it?"

Esau took a folded wad of official-looking documents from his jacket. "Here."

I hesitated to take the paper. I so distrusted Esau at the moment that the first thing I thought of was that he was handing me a subpoena or a summons.

He shook the paper at me. "Go ahead. It's all good."

I grabbed the sheets of paper and perused them. It was an itemized statement of what I owed Esau. The total was $9,423.06. Well—of all the gall!

"You've got some nerve, Esau Clay. I won't pay it! Not one red cent. You got me into this mess. I can't believe you would charge me so much. To think your mother and I used to play bridge together. I'm going to call her and tell her how you are mistreating me. You just used me."

"Oh, shut up, Josiah. Look at the last page."

I flipped to the last page where I saw the words printed in large letters.

BALANCE IS ZERO. ALL MEDICINE, PROCE-
DURES, AND APPOINTMENTS OF THE
ACCOUNT OF JOSIAH LOUISE REYNOLDS
HAVE BEEN WAIVED BY ESAU CLAY UNTIL
FURTHER NOTICE.

I clutched the bill to my chest. Relieved, I beamed at Esau and felt the world was lifted off my shoulders.

He was really a good boy, after all.

23

"Shaneika called me and told me what happened with the Trouts," Esau said.

"Oh, I see. You take Shaneika's calls, but won't return mine. Jeez."

Esau looked disheartened at first, but then chuckled. "You are too much, Jo. Look, I had no idea that things would get out of hand like they have. I also came to apologize because you've carried the brunt of my good intentions. I want to make it right."

"Then pay for the restoration of my stable door, my fences, and loss of income. I'll throw in the hay, sweet feed, and my aggravation, as well."

"Remember I was sued by the Trouts as well, Jo."

I was not deterred from complaining. "Oh, I had to pay Velvet Maddox three hundred dollars for her reading."

"That's cheap for Velvet. Must have felt sorry for you."

"I threw in a couple bottles of Kentucky bourbon

to sweeten the pie."

"I thought the police were going to pay for the reading."

"They never came through, and you know how Velvet wants her money ASAP. She'll reimburse me if she gets a check from the Madison County Police Department. I can trust her." I turned to Esau, staring at his freshly shaved face. He still looked like a teenager to me and not the handsome, dark-haired doctor of veterinary medicine. "Where have you been, Esau? I needed you."

"I want you to know that I have taken a financial hit on these animals, too. I had to hire a lawyer due to the Trout's lawsuit, and my bill with you is pro bono. That's a huge hit. I didn't mean to ghost you, but I've been really busy. I had planned to return your call."

"What a load of crap. Calls. It was calls—not a call." I parted my hair and bowed my head. "This is where Narcy Trout hit me with my own honey bottle. Did you see my twisted security gate? I have to replace it now and the cost is no chicken feed."

"You don't give a man much room to maneuver. All right, I was ducking you."

"The only reason you have voided my bill is because you feel guilty, but I'll take it because I deserve free vet services. Your vet bill is nothing compared to what I owe Shaneika Mary Todd because of these animals."

"Wow. Not even grateful one little bit. You are the

most ornery woman I've ever met. No disrespect, mind you."

Now that Esau had voided my bill, I was somewhat in a forgiving mood, willing to kiss and make up, so to speak. I playfully elbowed Esau in his ribs. "You know that's not true."

"You're right. I've met animal owners that make you look like a pussycat." Esau gave me a hard stare as though he was trying to figure me out. "You know, Josiah, most people would have handed these animals over in a heartbeat. They are smelly beasts that eat like a plague of locusts, but you stuck with them. You fed them, housed them, protected them. Might I even say—loved them."

"Look at Tex."

Esau followed my gaze.

"I mean really look at him. Tex is a magnificent creature—a symbol of the Old West. He's part of what makes us who we are today. Look at all these animals here. We need to keep these breeds alive and well. Make sure they have their place in the scheme of things. Doesn't matter if these animals pay for their keep. It's just a pleasure to look at them—to know that they are part of the Great Circle of Life. They have a right to exist without interference from humans."

"I agree, Josiah. I told you before I do what I can when I can for the rights of animals."

"The thing that puzzles me is all the interest Ulysses

Grant had in Tex. Why make Tex's life a misery? He seemed to have it out for this bull. Why?"

"I had always found Tex a handful. Perhaps he made Ulysses' life a misery."

I cast a suspicious glance at Esau. Wasn't he the one who told me that Tex was usually gentle? Now he was casting aspersions on Tex. Why was Esau changing his story?

"I think it odd that Grant was so fixated on Tex. It's obvious the bull was not producing like he should have been, and if he was difficult like you surmise, why not purchase a younger Texas Longhorn bull? Why keep Tex around?"

"I don't know the answer." He pulled a cough drop out of his pocket and unwrapped it, popping it into his mouth.

I held out my hand for one.

Esau produced another lozenge—cherry this time.

I said, "Ulysses Grant was in the business of animal breeding—if not natural then by artificial insemination. Animals that don't yield money are taken to the slaughterhouse. I didn't know the man but that's the way of his business. Why didn't he give Tex the boot?"

"You sound critical. You're in the agricultural business. One would think you would be less judgmental about Ulysses Grant."

"I'm in the business of keeping honeybees alive. I'm in the business of lodging horses. I don't kill animals in order to make a living."

"But you eat them."

"Yes, that's why I'm having such a difficult time with these animals. I eat beef. I eat chicken. That Belgian Blue was scientifically engineered for the beef industry. His flesh could feed a family of six an entire winter. I know we need animal protein to survive, but I don't think I could give these animals up to the abattoir." I pointed at the Longhorns. "They have such distinct personalities."

Esau asked, "Have you talked with Cary Grant?"

"He said he doesn't want them, but he'll change his mind. There's too much money on the hoof here." I threw an apple into the pasture. Tex ambled over and snatched it up in one bite. "When did you speak with the son?"

Ignoring my question, Esau said, "Shaneika mentioned he had won his father's estate. The rumor in town is that he is going to sell the farm to a developer."

I shuddered as I hated the thought that more prime Bluegrass land was going to be paved over with tacky tract-houses. "Did Shaneika tell you about the Trouts making a last minute attempt the steal the creatures?"

"Yeah, she brought me up-to-date."

"Why are you really here, Esau?"

"So, to answer your question, Cary Grant called me this morning. You are right. He's changed his mind about the critters. He wants them now. I'm here to break the news to you."

I took a deep breath and slowly let it out.

Didn't I warn you that Cary Grant would want the animals back?

24

I didn't understand why Esau was acting as Cary's messenger boy. The younger Mr. Grant could have called me himself. He had my contact information. I told Esau that I would call Grant and settle the matter. It was just to get rid of him. I was deeply suspicious of Esau now. He had been ignoring my calls and then suddenly showed up with a voided bill only after he admits to speaking with Cary Grant. He could have told me that he voided my vet bill on the phone. Why had Esau avoided me? And why was he changing his story about Tex's disposition?

I hurried over to Lady Elsmere's Big House and entered the kitchen like I always do. "June up?" I asked as I snatched a lemon bar off the marble-topped island.

"I'm making her elevenses."

"The lemon bars are really good."

Bess gave me a quick smile. She loved flattery. I don't know why as everyone knows she is the best cook in the county and perhaps the entire South. Many a millionaire and billionaire had tried to whisk her away from Lady Elsmere, but Bess stayed loyal to June. It might be that Bess' family inheriting June's estate after she passes to the Great Beyond might have something to do with her decision.

Remember me talking about Esau being a descendant of Henry Clay? Well, the father of Bess is Charles Dupuy, a direct descendant of Aaron Dupuy, who was Henry Clay's boyhood friend and also his slave. This is why people in the South ask, "Who are your people?" That's because everyone here is connected somehow.

Aaron Dupuy's wife was Charlotte Dupuy, and she was one of the first slaves to sue for her freedom. She lost, and Henry Clay sent Charlotte deep into the South as punishment. That's a lot of history for one family.

Charles began work as a butler for Lady Elsmere and quickly moved into management. I credit myself with Her Ladyship leaving the Dupuys her estate. She has to leave her property and monies to someone as she has no direct heirs. I certainly didn't want the responsibility of running her little empire. Why not the Dupuys who had worked loyally for Lady Elsmere the last quarter of her life? They were good, decent people and deserved a leg up because their ancestors didn't get any great shakes. They certainly had proven that they were up to the task.

"I need some eggs, Josiah. Bring me three dozen today. I've only got two eggs left."

"If you make those eggs scrambled with some toast served with your homemade strawberry jelly, I'll give you four dozen eggs."

Bess put on her apron. "Skillet—make way for some eggs." She flashed a spatula at me. "Take Miss June's tray, and I'll bring your eggs up when done."

I picked up a tray of lemon bars, cinnamon rolls nicely diced into small squares, sliced apples, tangerine segments, and a nice big pot of tea. Making my way to the elevator, I almost dropped the tray but corrected myself in time. Finally, I landed on the second floor, but had to kick open June's door with my foot. "Good morning," I said to June, sitting upright in bed like a pasha wearing a pink cashmere shawl and silver brocade turban with one of her priceless emerald brooches pinned to the front.

"Good morning," June answered, looking greedily at the tray, which was placed over her lap.

"Why are you still in bed?" I asked, detecting the odor of cigarette smoke. I knew June had tucked a pack under the satin quilt when she heard me coming.

"Because I feel like it. No appointments today."

"Some of your friends might drop by, and here you sit with no makeup and not dressed. Whatever will they think?" I teased in an upper-class accent and pushed back my upper lip to exaggerate a toothy grin. I always joked that June's rich friends, who had bought Thoroughbred farms in Lexington, looked like horses themselves, suggesting inbreeding of the East Coast upper class.

"Oh, quit nagging me like an ill-tempered mother-in-law."

I sat on the bed and snagged a lemon bar. "Gosh, these are good."

June smacked my hand as I reached for another lemon bar. "This is my tray. Get your own."

"Bess is making me breakfast," I replied as I poured tea for Her Ladyship. "No need to get so huffy. You *are* in a sour mood this morning."

As June didn't want to continue this conversation, she segued, "Where is Baby? He hasn't visited me for a week."

"Baby is staying with Detective Kelly. I guess I'll pick him up today."

"Hasn't gone well for you this week, has it?"

"Nope, everything has gone dismally wrong. I couldn't have been a bigger fool if I tried."

"I heard the charges against Echo Trout were dismissed."

"There are still charges against Narcy Trout pending." I grabbed a couple of apple slices and munched on them. "What would you do if you were me, June?"

"The animals have a forever home at my sanctuary if you can procure their ownership. However, I can't keep the animals if they are allowed to breed."

"I thought you wanted these animals to procreate to

keep the breeds going."

'Oh, I do, but the sanctuary only has so much room. I know of a couple of young girls who would love to take the Valais Blacknose sheep for a 4-H project. They are interested in wool production. Besides, the sheep are so cute, these gals would be delighted to take care of them just as pets. The sheep would have a happy home."

"And the others?"

"We'll find someone to help with the Rove goats. The bulls can stay where they are. I don't think Tex is up to romance anymore, and the Belgian Blue can retire from being a stud."

Bess entered the room bringing my breakfast tray. She placed it on the bed. "You two solve the world's problems this morning?"

"There are no problems when I eat your cooking, Bess," I said, staring at my scrambled eggs cooked to perfection with dry toast boasting a lump of strawberry jam, sliced oranges, orange juice, hot tea, and several lemon bars thrown on the plate for added color. "A veritable feast, my good woman."

Beaming, Bess wiped her hands on a white starched apron. It was a well-known fact that Bess couldn't abide a dirty apron and changed hers frequently throughout the day. "Hey, where's that mangy dog of yours been? I haven't seen Baby for days."

"You'll see him tomorrow showing up at your back

kitchen door begging for treats."

Bess rolled her eyes. "Oh, I can't wait."

"I know you love my dog, Bess. I know you do."

"Oh, get on. Who can stand that filthy mess but you?"

"I know you miss Baby," I teased, turning to Lady Elsmere. "Doesn't she, June?"

Bess said, "You're impossible, Josiah. Enjoy your breakfast and don't forget to bring those five dozen eggs."

"Five dozen eggs?" I echoed. "When did it become five dozen eggs?"

Bess waved my concern away and turned to leave, saying, "You heard me."

I didn't reply because I was too busy stuffing my face while making a mental plan for the day: pick up Baby, move my animals home, transfer my boarded mares from Lady Elsmere's farm to mine, bring Bess her eggs, and call Cary Grant. He was last on my list as I needed time to formulate a plan. Was I to reason with him? Offer to purchase the animals? Ignore him and lie that Esau did not relay the message from Cary to me? Or should I visit Detective Lucas McCain instead?

I poured June another cup of tea before munching contentedly on my breakfast feast. I ate my meal slowly while thinking absentmindedly.

Putting her cup down and frustrated that I wasn't jabbering, June asked, "What's on your mind, Josiah?"

"I'm just pondering on what to do next."

"Does Detective McCain think Tex had anything to do with Ulysses Grant's murder?"

"I'm not in the man's confidence. The only thing I know is that there hasn't been an arrest. I don't even know what the coroner finally submitted on the death certificate. The paper did say that Detective McCain made the coroner take another look at the body, but didn't state the conclusion."

"Looks like you're up the creek without a paddle."

"June, all the pieces are there. I just don't know how the pieces fit together."

"Do what you do with a physical puzzle. Shake the box up. Then maybe you will find the one piece that fits the magic spot and makes sense of the rest."

"Shake the box up, huh?"

"What can the police or the Trouts do to you?"

"I can think of several unpleasant things. I could get sued by Cary Grant, get thrown into jail by McCain for interfering, or have the Trouts pull another whammy on me. I've not been very successful with those siblings."

"Mere trifles," June sniffed. "Mere trifles."

I knew Her Ladyship was trying to motivate me, but at the moment I wanted to eat my breakfast, then gather Baby, and go home. I didn't want to recount my failures.

I wanted normalcy, but I wasn't going to get it.

25

I knocked on Kelly's front door, which was opened by screaming kids cavorting with my English Mastiff. Baby was wearing a faux-diamond tiara clipped lopsided to one ear and a feathered boa roped around his neck.

I tried not to laugh as Baby looked relieved to see me. I think he'd had too much of a good thing, ready for the relative serenity of the Butterfly and the company of the Kitty Kaboodle Gang.

Kelly's children gave Baby one last fierce hug while he stood patiently with his massive tongue dripping drool on the floor. I wiped his face and the floor with a towel, said goodbye to the excited Kelly offspring, and thanked their parents profusely. As we left, Kelly shut the door a little forcefully—almost like a slam. I think Kelly and his wife were ready for a little quiet.

Baby ran to my VW van and jumped into the front seat without a command. He watched me make my way around to the driver's side and gave a quick yelp.

"I'm coming. I'm coming, Baby."

Once inside the van and sitting, he sniffed me profusely. Where had I been without him? Whom had I seen? I pushed his nose away. "Behave, Baby. You haven't missed much."

Baby gave me one last long sniff and then sneezed.

"Bless you," I said, turning the key. It was then that an epiphany hit me. "How could I be so stupid?" I said out loud.

Baby cocked his head the way dogs do when trying to understand.

"Let's get home, Baby. We've some sleuthing to do." I pulled out of Kelly's driveway feeling better than I had in weeks.

26

"I don't understand why you need this," Mike said, "but you can borrow it if you must."

"This wand picks up any electronic device like a computer chip?" I asked.

"Yes, we chip all our horses now in case they get lost or stolen. However, the chips are not GPS trackers. They won't help you find an animal—just ID it. If you want to keep track of a pet, you must use a GPS tracker."

"Understand. Do you still tattoo the upper lip of Thoroughbreds?"

"Not as much anymore. We chip and take pictures of the horse's coat."

I said, "I don't understand."

"Each horse's coat is unique, like a fingerprint. We photograph scars, swirls, and unusual patterns on a horse's coat. Including the chip, it gives us extra identification. Of course, anyone can insert a chip and provide false information. It's the size of a grain of rice and has a finite life span."

"Besides the ID of the animal's owner, what else does the chip do?"

"This technology is used mostly in companion animals like dogs and cats. However, in the next five years, more information will be stored on a chip."

"Like what?" I asked.

"Complete ownership provenance, weight, medications, vaccinations, operations, feed requirements, behavioral issues associated with the animal. Lots of information."

"How is the information stored on a chip and who puts it there?"

Mike explained, "You can buy trackers and chips now at most agricultural or general retail stores on the internet. Are you worried about the bulls? I know with cattle, GPS tags are clipped on their ears."

"But for a more sophisticated chip with reams of information stored on it—who could do that?"

"Someone with a computer degree or any fourteen-year-old nerd who has the right equipment."

"And how are they injected into the animal?"

Mike looked at me with a surprised expression. "You mean Esau Clay hasn't chipped your animals? Baby is not chipped?"

I shook my head. "I really don't know, Mike. I never asked about it as I never sell my critters, and Esau never mentioned it. He may have."

Narrowing his eyebrows in dismay, Mike said, "I think that is downright negligent. You need to get Baby chipped. The chip is injected under the skin with a syringe. Doesn't hurt them."

"Where?"

"Mostly behind an ear or on the back behind the neck. Really depends on the animal." Mike shifted his weight. "You need to get Baby chipped."

"I want to check my animals, which is why I need the chip scanner. So, can I borrow this wand?"

"Yes, but bring it back. We only have an extra one. One more thing, chips can travel on the body."

"Didn't know that."

"Make sure you return the scanner."

"Will do. Thanks, Mike."

I took the scanner wand and hurried away before Mike would ask more questions. I didn't want to explain my theory. I had already looked like a fool, and I didn't want to add fuel to the fire.

What I was thinking was a long shot, after all—shaking the puzzle box.

27

I entered the Valais Blacknose sheep pasture with a bucket of grain. Since my own rescued sheep were intermingled with them, I was quickly surrounded by sheep nudging me. They smelled the cracked corn. I was happy to oblige but I didn't like being pushed around by the older ewes. Goodness, they were demanding. I dumped the feed out and as they circled around me, I waved the wand over their bodies. Except for the lambs and my sheep, all of Ulysses Grant's sheep had been chipped. The wand really worked.

I now summoned my courage up to try to scan the Belgian Blue bull. Climbing up on the fence and sitting on the rim of the plank, I called to him, offering an apple. He lumbered over with his lady friend and her calf. I wasn't as cautious of him as I was of Tex. Since he seemed like a big gentle baby, I pulled the bull's halter to position him sideways to the fence. He complied as soon as I held out another apple and while he was munching on it, I waved the wand. He too was chipped. The wand displayed Ulysses Grant's name, phone number, and address.

"Good boy," I said, scratching him behind the ear. He bumped into the fence wanting to get closer and almost knocked me off my perch. I grabbed the fence post to steady myself. "You are a big boy, aren't you?" I gave him a good scratching behind both his ears. Happy with the attention, the Belgian Blue was so tall that he laid his heavy head on my lap so I could pet his muzzle. I held onto a post with one hand while petting him and finally pushed his head away. "Enough now. You're not the one I'm looking for." Before gingerly climbing down, I tossed about five more apples into the pasture for the cow and calf as well. The distraction worked well and the bull moved away from the fence.

"Well, it's now or never," I muttered. Working up my nerve, I walked over to Tex's pasture. Even though Tex had not shown any signs of aggression for weeks, it startled me when I discovered him right by the fence line watching me interact with the Belgian Blues. Tex's horns clicked against the wooden planks as he moved his head between the planks to get a better view.

While Tex had behaved recently, he still was dangerous. His demeanor was so different from that of the larger, but more tame Belgian Blues. Truth be told, I was very wary of the Texas Longhorn and those deadly horns.

I baby-talked to Tex and thrust an apple through

the space between the planks. He gently took it from my palm and munched contentedly as I climbed the fence and balanced myself on the rim of the top plank. I held up another apple. "Tex. Tex. Look at me. Look at me."

Tex raised his head with those horns swinging dangerously close to me.

I waved the wand over his head and withers which caused Tex to stomp and push against the fence. I dropped several apples causing Tex to lower his head to eat, but because of his horns he had to step away from the fence. That meant I had to lean dangerously over to pass the wand above him. I wanted him to sidle next to the fence, but how does one pull a two thousand pound, cranky bull into position. I certainly didn't want to tug on his horns. Precariously holding onto the fence post and leaning just enough to wave the wand, but not fall onto Tex's head was an acrobatic feat which I was surprised I could still manage.

I got two beeps but I couldn't read the codes on the device in my outstretched hand. I would have to get closer with Tex. You know there is a fine line between being brave and just plain stupid. Too often I get close to the latter.

I climbed down the fence, opened the gate to the field, got into my golf cart, and drove into the pasture. He and his ladylove slowly plodded over with Tex tossing his head up and down. I knew that meant he was suspicious of me being inside his domain.

My hand trembled as I threw out more treats, hoping my three pound bag of Gala apples would last. "Come on, Tex. Be a good lad," I muttered. "Let me scan you, big fellow." I trusted that Tex's love of apples would outweigh his distrust of the golf cart and me.

I was frightened. If Tex had a mind to, he could tip my cart over and then take his massive horns to decimate it. He loved tearing things up.

Tex came over and stuck his nose inside the cart and sniffed. I immediately thrust an apple under his nose. He sniffed again and then took the apple, crunching loudly and dropping apple bits into my lap, something I was accustomed to with Baby leaving bits of his cookies. The difference was that Baby didn't weigh close to two thousand pounds.

His mate bellowed at being left out, so I threw an apple out for her.

I needed Tex to move sideways for me, so I threw five apples about ten feet from me. Tex followed the apples. I slowly got out of the cart and dumped sweet feed on the ground near the apples. Tex snorted and moved to the feed as he smelled the molasses. I knew he was a sweet fanatic and could be sidelined with this treat. As he bowed his head to munch on his feast, I slowly sidled closer to him.

Tex gave me a sidelong glance but didn't move except to shift his weight.

ABIGAIL KEAM

I gradually raised my hand and scanned his back. First beep. I took a picture of the information on the wand's screen with my phone. Then I scanned his left shoulder. Got another beep and took a picture of the information flashing on the wand's screen. The screen was small on the wand, but I could see it was a mass of numbers. Just to be sure, I scanned his head.

Noticing the wand in his peripheral vision, Tex kicked and shook his head, giving me a stern warning.

I slowly backed up, got into my cart, and drove out of the field as fast as my little golf cart would go.

Tex watched me leave and bellowed loudly.

I dumped the rest of the apples and sweet feed by the fence. "Thank you, Tex. You are a good fellow."

I was now convinced that Tex had nothing to do with Ulysses Grant's death. Like I said before, cattle act differently from horses or sheep, but they have distinct personalities, just like any animal. Once you know their behavior patterns, their actions are predictable. Tex showed me he could be gentled with food, and he only acted aggressively when he saw the wand near his head. I think he thought the wand might be a cattle prod and became frightened.

The Longhorn's conduct proved what I was saying. Tex was not dangerous when handled correctly. One just had to be patient and have lots of cow delicacies handy.

Now that I knew Tex had two chips, I wanted to

know what information was stored on the second chip. I needed someone to interpret the info, but who?

Ah, yes, I knew of a person who had a computer software degree and knew coding. My favorite geek.

Franklin!

28

I handed the scanner to Franklin. "Can you take a peek at the information on this wand and tell me what it means?" We were in his living room where Franklin had his work desk.

Franklin turned the wand over and studied the buttons. "This is part of an information system that ranchers use to keep track of their cattle. It's one of the newer systems on the market. This company provides the chips, scanner, and software program."

"Just cattle?"

Sitting back in his chair, Franklin explained, "It can be used for any herd, but it was designed specifically for cattle."

"Lady Elsmere has this program for her horses."

"Horses are herd animals, Josiah."

Matt came out of the kitchen with a tray of cheese, crackers, and olives. "What do you want to drink, Josiah?"

"A cup of hot tea would be nice."

"Coming up." Matt went back into the kitchen while Franklin studied the wand.

"Where's Emmeline?"

Franklin answered, "She's at the daycare up the street for a couple of hours every day. Otherwise, she gets fussy. I think she's turning into a social butterfly."

"I'm sorry I missed her."

Matt brought out a mug of hot tea and placed it on the coffee table in front of me. "Here you go. Sugar?"

"No, thank you."

Matt sat down beside me.

"Why aren't you two at work?" I asked.

"We decided to take a long weekend and do fun stuff," Matt said. "How is my house in the country?"

"It's fine. Waiting for your return. I think most of the drama is over."

"For the time being," Matt remarked, looking away.

I didn't like Matt's tone and wondered if he had grown tired of being around the chaos that is my life. I resolved if that he decided to move on, I would be a champ about it. He had a baby to think of and that meant no matter how much Matt loved me, his priorities were different now. I understood.

Turning to Franklin, I said, "Well?"

"We can purchase the program and then download the data from the wand into it."

"Okay, let's do it."

"It's a very expensive program, Jo. You will have to

pay for it. Better yet, why don't you download the information into Lady Elsmere's program?"

"I don't want to further involve her."

"Okay. Then purchase the program. We can install it now."

"Right. How much?"

When Franklin told me the amount, I was floored. "For a cattle program?"

"Yep."

"Can I transfer this program to my computer and use it for my other animals?" I asked.

"I do believe so if they are chipped."

"You said the company provides the chips."

"Yes, they do and with the syringe to insert the chips."

"How do I put my information on the chips?" I was very curious about this entire chipping process.

"You will fill out these fields with your information and the company will send the chips with the information coded on them—or they can send you blank chips and you code your own information on them—if you know how."

"Which I don't."

"There are instructions or I can do it for you. It's relatively simple."

"For you, maybe." I took a sip of tea before making a decision. I had lost a fair amount of income the past month which I was never going to recoup. It made me

hesitate. The good angel on my right shoulder whispered, *You've got money in the bank. You're being stingy and
cheap.*

I said, "Let's get it then. I'll write you a check before
I leave and deduct it as a farm expense." Who am I to
ignore the prodding of sweet angels entreating my
better nature?

"Okey-dokey. Here we go." Franklin clicked on a
link, purchased the program, and installed it on his
computer. It only took a few moments to set up the
passwords and read the instructions. I must say
Franklin is a wizard when it comes to computers. He
did in twenty minutes what would have taken me
hours, not to mention the frustration and gnashing of
teeth. When all the security and personal information
fields were filled, Franklin plugged in the wand. He
brought up the data contained on the first chip. It was
general information about Tex as to his owner, address,
phone number, and place of origin. It also had information about Tex's first owner. Seems like Ulysses had
purchased him as a calf from another breeding farm in
Tennessee. Tex was five years old.

"Anything else?" I asked.

Franklin swung around in his swivel chair. "That's it
for that one. Let's try this second chip listed." Franklin
typed on his keyboard and clicked on a few buttons on
the screen. Suddenly, ones and zeros in six-digit
sequences filled the computer screen.

Both Matt and I pulled up chairs close to the computer.

"What is that?" I asked.

"Is it binary coding?" Matt asked.

Franklin shook his head. "No, because it seems to be in a sequence of six numbers each. The spacing between the numbers is wrong for binary coding, but just to be sure—." Franklin copied the numbers and fed them into one of his binary programs on another computer. Nothing but gibberish appeared on the screen.

"Fortran, maybe?" I suggested.

Franklin shook his head.

"What about coordinates?" I suggested.

Both Matt and Franklin nixed that idea.

"Longitude and latitude use numbers higher than zero and one," Matt replied.

"Any ideas, fellows?" I asked, biting my thumb nail while thinking.

Franklin offered, "I think these numbers are some sort of code but of what I have no idea."

"Where do we go from here?" I asked.

"I have some cipher programs. Why don't you let me have a go at them? May take some time though. Matt and I want to visit with the baby before we go back to work on Monday. Next Wednesday okay to get back with you?"

"That's fine and Franklin—I want to pay you for this."

He waved the idea away. "Just pay for the program before you leave."

"No, really, I'm going to pay you for your time as well."

Matt intervened. "Franklin, take the money or Josiah will pester you to death. She hates to owe anybody."

"Okay, then it's settled. I should be finished by Wednesday. I will call you when I'm done though."

"Sounds like a plan," I said, agreeing.

Matt asked, "If you stick around for an early dinner, you can go with me to pick up Emmeline. We put her to bed at six-thirty. I'm not saying she goes to sleep, but we put her to bed then."

"I would like that, Matt. Thank you."

"Where's Baby?" Franklin asked.

"He's in the car waiting for me."

"I'm sure he needs to tinkle. Is there a leash in the car?"

"Yes."

"I'll take care of Baby and start dinner. You two pick up Emmeline."

Matt stood and gathered his jacket. Like two old friends, we walked to the day care center not saying a word along the way. There was no need to speak. We understood each other.

We picked up Emmeline and once we got back to Franklin's apartment, I changed her day clothes into pajamas, washed her face, and read her several stories while Matt and Franklin prepared our dinner and Emmeline's as well. She was eating solid food now, and I sat next to her at the table trying to feed the little monster. Most of her food spilled out onto her jammies and on the floor. She apparently didn't like peas or applesauce or cauliflower mashed potatoes. She kept grabbing for my food which was getting cold.

I finally gathered Emmeline and took her into the guest bedroom where Matt had set up a crib. I laid the baby on the adult bed and snuggled close reading some of her favorite stories while she munched on saltine crackers. Saltine crackers were the best a parent could do some nights. Her face and hands were sticky with cracker residue but I was not going to clean her as she was becoming drowsy. As soon as Emmeline's eyes closed and her breathing became rhythmic, I put the sticky and crusty baby in the crib. I made sure the baby monitor was on before I left the room.

Coming back into the kitchen alcove, I sat down. "Where's the mess that Emmeline made?"

Franklin laughed. "Baby cleaned it up. He's better than a vacuum cleaner."

"He's good for cleaning up food spills, that's for sure."

Both Matt and Franklin had finished their grilled steak dinners and had cleared their places at the table.

"Thanks for taking care of Emmeline," Matt said.

"My pleasure. She's awfully messy, though."

Matt assured me. "I'll clean her up tomorrow morning."

Both Matt and Franklin looked expectantly at me.

I took the hint. "It's been a long day. I'm really tired. Would you excuse me, boys? I think I'll hurry home."

"Are you sure?" Franklin asked. "You haven't had anything to eat."

"I'll be fine. Thank you for the invitation and taking the time to see me on such short notice. I know you both are very busy."

"I'll call you when I discover something," Franklin said.

"Until then, au revoir," I said as I gathered my purse.

You know that old saying—"What's your hurry? Here's your hat." I was definitely getting the bum's rush by those two. I wondered what was going on. Something was brewing. I could feel it. Were they getting back together? If yes, then I feared for Franklin, but it was none of my business.

I guess I would find out sooner or later. I called my dog. "Come on, Baby. Let's go home."

And we did—without incident.

29

The next day, Baby and I went to work at the farmers' market. Lincoln Todd, that's Shaneika's son, helped me set up. His mother's office is right across the square, so Lincoln comes with her on Saturday morning where she works for a couple of hours. They have an early breakfast, and then Lincoln comes over to help me set up so he can make a little pin money. We call him Linc for short.

I gave sideways glances at Lincoln. He was entering a growing stage—he was taller, his facial bones were lengthening, and his hands were all outsized fingers and thumbs—meaning he was beginning his way toward becoming a preteen. It wouldn't be long now before he'd tower over my head. I was going to miss that little boy, but growing up was the way of the world.

"How's Morning Glory doing?" Linc asked, lining up honey by color into rows on my table.

I had given Morning Glory over to Lincoln as I was not a good rider like he was. Morning Glory needed more companionship than I could offer and Linc loved horses. It was a good match. "She needs to be exercised. Coming to ride her soon?"

"This afternoon. Mom is helping Grandma set up the Butterfly."

"Ah, yes, I forgot. We are throwing a small wedding reception this evening at the Butterfly. Just twelve people. Sure, come on."

Lincoln offered a glorious grin consisting of straight, white teeth. No braces would be needed for this child. His smile made me feel all squishy inside. It's so nice when children are happy and animals desire our attention—the way Baby was at the moment. "Just a minute, Baby."

Baby smelled dog biscuits in my pockets and wanted one. I didn't have time to bother with him as one of my early regular customers approached the table. She petted Baby on the head, as he gulped back saliva, allowing his massive tongue to hang out of his mouth while panting. I saw the customer sneak Baby a small dog cookie when she thought I wasn't looking. Baby licked his mouth and nudged the customer's pocket. "Sorry, Baby. No more today," the customer said, handing me money for two honey bottles.

"Don't be a pest, Baby," I scolded. "He's a chow hound, I'm afraid."

The customer said, "Don't worry. Everyone loves your dog."

Lincoln grabbed Baby's collar and pulled him away from the customer. He tugged Baby around to the bed I had brought for him. "Now, stay," Linc said forcefully. "I need to buy things for Mom. When I go, you can come with me, but for now stay in your bed."

As if understanding what Lincoln was saying, Baby sneezed, circled three times, and then lay in his makeshift bed.

"If that don't beat all," the customer responded. "Like Baby understood everything Lincoln uttered."

I didn't have time to respond as all three of us heard the guttural roar of a loud car motor. The sound was deafening. Baby howled in distress. Lincoln, the customer, and I turned toward the sound when my heart froze. The vehicle was a red muscle car with a falcon emblazoned on the hood.

So Jimmy J had found me at last.

30

I quickly gave the customer her change and thanked her. As soon as she was out of earshot, I said to Lincoln, "I want you to give your mother a message. It's very important."

Lincoln looked eager. "What is it?"

"Tell her that Jimmy J just arrived. He's here."

"That's all?"

"That's enough. I want you to tell her now and no lollygagging. You go straight to her office right away. Understand?"

"Sure."

"Go now and don't come back to the market. Go, Linc. Go."

After giving me a queer look, Lincoln started for his mother's office. I saw him cross the street and disappear into his mother's building. A few minutes later, Shaneika appeared at the window, scanning for Jimmy J's car. When she spied me, she gave me a thumbs up.

I returned the gesture. Then I called Detective Kelly

and left a message. For the next ten minutes my eyes darted every which way until I observed a uniformed policeman casually walking through the market. He strolled past a man leaning against a pillar eating an heirloom tomato across from my booth.

The man watched the officer pass by and catching my eye, smirked, obviously trying to gain my attention. He was a lanky man in his late thirties with a three day stubble and scruffy brown hair. Wearing ripped jeans, a *ZZ Top* tee-shirt with the sleeves cut off, and worn cowboy boots, he exuded the "bad boy" vibe. Oh, there were tattoos on his arms as well. I hate to say this, but he was sexy in a slimy way—a Stanley Kowalski for the modern age. This had to be Jimmy J.

The man's eyes lingered on me until he slid a finger across his throat and mouthed, *You're next.*

31

I know I shouldn't have, but I burst out laughing. This guy must have watched too many gangster movies. No one does this in real life. I picked up my phone and stood within ten feet of the man I thought was Jimmy J, turning on my video app.

"Hey, Jimmy J. Do that again where you act as though you're cutting my throat. Were you threatening me?"

"I don't know what you're talking about, stupid old woman." He substituted another word for woman but let's be tasteful here.

"Not going to threaten me again? Ah, come on. A crowd is here. They would love to see you impersonating Al Capone—or should I say a weak attempt of him."

"Who? Who's this Al Capone?"

"A real gangster. Not a wannabe."

A small crowd gathered and one of my customers at the market stood next to me. "What did he say, Josiah? Did he threaten you?"

I pointed to Jimmy J. "This is Jimmy Ray Jones."

Looking intently at Jimmy J, she said, "Oh, a serial-killer name."

"That's what I say. His nickname is Jimmy J, and he pantomimed cutting my throat just a few minutes ago."

The woman glared at Jimmy J. "That's not nice, young man. Josiah has put seventeen people behind bars who tangled with her. I don't know what your beef is, but you were licked even before you started."

Embarrassed and angry, Jimmy J threw down his tomato smashing it on the pavement. Giving the crowd a look of disdain, he stormed off.

My laughter and the crowd's derision followed.

The uniformed policeman pursued him as did Detective Kelly wearing plain clothes. Hmm? When did Kelly show up?

I glanced at Shaneika's building and could see her videoing Jimmy J's departure from her third floor window. I went back to my table where I found Baby napping in his bed and scolded, "Great help you were."

He opened his one good eye and suddenly sat up looking about as if to say, *What did I miss?*

Hearing the loud rumbling of his hot rod engine zoom past the market, I witnessed Jimmy J's red muscle car speed by.

One thing I knew for sure. If that boy was going to sneak up on me again, he was going to have to rid himself of that earsplitting speedster.

It was a dead giveaway.

32

It's not that I am recalcitrant. It's that so many people throughout my life have told me I was wrong when it turned out that I was right—so I follow my own lead now. More often than not, following my gut has led me in the right direction. If I had done that when I was younger, it would have saved me a lot of money and heartache, especially with my late husband.

So I went to Cary Grant's business unannounced to strike a deal. He was standing at the customer counter when I strolled in. Grant looked up in surprise and then gave a quick smile. "You here to make arrangements to give me back Dad's animals?"

"I'm here to talk to you about them," I replied.

"Okay. Give me a moment."

He finished helping a customer and gave the counter over to one of his employees. "Let's go into my office."

I followed Grant into his office and was pointed to a chair while he went to one behind his desk. "Would you like something to drink?"

"No, thank you."

Before I could speak further, the man asked, "When are you bringing the animals?"

"Mr. Grant, there is the matter of their upkeep and damage to my farm."

Grant's smile faded. "That's not my problem. Those animals were taken without my consent."

"It is your problem, sir, if I make it so. A lawsuit would tie you up for a long time and cost you money in lawyer fees. I can defend my position as pictures were taken of the animals when they came into my possession. They looked less than stellar. There's also the damage caused by Tex who originally wandered onto my property and started this mess. Your father's estate is responsible for correcting this. And to mention last, Esau Clay's vet bill."

Grant narrowed his eyes. "What are you trying to pull? I know for a fact that Esau Clay had voided his vet bill."

So it was true that Esau had made some sort of deal with Cary Grant. That's why he was changing his story about Tex's demeanor. I pushed on. "There is still the matter of the animals' feed. Here is my bill." I held up the invoice. "Also, your cousins caused me a great deal of trouble and lawyer fees. I'm not going to eat that."

"You take that up with them."

"I'm taking it up with you."

Grant stood up in a rush. "Lady, you get out of my office. I don't take kindly to threats."

I motioned him to sit. "Calm down, Mr. Grant. I'm here to negotiate a deal."

Grant took his seat again, albeit reluctantly. He was not a man to take orders, but saw it in his best interest to do so at the moment.

"What do you have in mind?"

"I want the animals. Give them to me, and I will void any cost of damage or upkeep since they have been with me. You will be free of them. What do you say?" I held out my hand to shake.

Grant leaned back in his chair and swiveled a bit. "No."

I pulled my hand away. "NO!? But Mr. Grant, it is a win-win for you. As you said previously, you are not in the livestock business."

"I want them and you're gonna get another lawsuit smacked on your head if you don't return them to me."

I'm sure that smacking remark was in reference to Narcy Trout hitting me on the head. "Then I withdraw my offer to tear up their feed and damage bill. Until that invoice is paid in full, I will take the animals in payment." I threw the invoice on the top of his desk. I was irritated beyond belief and sick of threats of lawsuits. He threatened me. Then I threatened him. It was childish to be sure.

I stood up in a huff. "And Mr. Grant."

"What?" he asked gruffly.

"I found two chips on Tex. I retrieved the information on both."

"Two chips?" He didn't look all that surprised.

"One had some sort of suspicious code on it. I turned the information over to the police, and they are working on it." Now that was a big, fat lie, but this man didn't know it.

Grant's eyes widened.

"And I think your father was killed over that information. I think Jimmy J has something to do with it, too." I gave a sweet smile. "Once the police decode the cipher, I'm sure they will be knocking on your door. Good day, sir."

I swept out of Grant's office, knowing I had hit a nerve.

It felt good.

33

I was across the street, filling up Franklin's tiny smart car with gas, when I spied Cary Grant tear out of his business in his green pickup truck. I had traded cars for my trip to see Cary Grant with Franklin as he needed my VW van to pick up a chest he had purchased. Where was the son of Ulysses Grant going so fast? Was it due to what I had uttered in his office?

Only one way to find out. I stopped pumping and closed the gas tank before jumping into the teeny car. I followed at a discreet distance until he turned onto a country lane. It would be hard to follow Grant on that curvy, winding road, so I pulled over on a hunch and plugged Narcy Trout's address that she had recited in court into the car's GPS. Oh, gosh. My hunch was correct. He was going to her home. Well, don't that beat all.

Since I knew where Narcy lived, I could sneak up on them and take some pictures. I don't know what that would prove. After all, they were cousins, but who knows. I gave him about a five minute head start before I began following again. I drove slowly scouting people's driveways for the green pickup. This was a country lane with farmhouses along both sides of the road. It was easy to see if he had stopped at one of the houses. He hadn't. I kept going toward the address I had for Narcy, but many of the mailboxes by the road didn't have names or address numbers. It was slow going searching for the green pickup.

Finally, I came to a trailer park in the middle of no-where. Looking at my phone, I discovered this was Narcy's address so I turned right. It was a huge trailer park with close to one hundred doublewides and mobile homes dotting the park. I made the various loops until I spotted Grant's truck parked alongside several other cars including a red muscle car with a falcon painted on the hood.

Oh, great. Jimmy J was here, too. I pulled over on the road about four spaces away from Narcy's and watched her trailer. After five minutes I heard shouting coming from the Narcy's doublewide. I started the car and pulled up to the trailer, lowered the passenger's window, and recorded their arguing. The only problem was that I couldn't make out what anyone was saying. Figuring no one would see me since they were occu-pied with each other, I sneaked out of the car and scampered to the side of the mobile home where a window was open and held up my phone to record. I occasionally took a quick peek standing on my tiptoes, but I couldn't do it very often.

Apparently, Cary Grant had told them about my visit and that I had discovered a second chip on Tex. "What kind of mischief did you involve my father in?"

"We did nothing but try to help your father after he had his stroke. You certainly weren't around," Narcy said.

"I was around and I don't think you did anything but help yourselves at my father's expense," Grant accused. He turned to Jimmy J. "What's your involvement in this?"

"Just a casual bystander. I sometimes accompanied Echo to your father's home," answered Jimmy J, tying his long hair into a knot. "You said a second chip was found on the Longhorn?"

"What's that to you? Why would you be interested in a cattle chip implanted inside a Longhorn bull?" Grant asked.

"Just making casual conversation, man. That's all."

Grant accused, "I think one of you hurt my father and the rest are covering up. Which one of you &**#% killed my father?"

"You're talking nonsense, Cary," Narcy said. "Uncle Ulysses was gored by Tex."

"The police don't think so now. I understand the coroner is going to change cause of death on Dad's death certificate to homicide."

Narcy and Echo exchanged frightened glances while Jimmy J calmly flipped open his Zippo lighter and lit a cigarette.

Grant continued, "That's not all. The Reynolds woman visited my office not more than an hour ago and claims the second chip on Tex had some weird code on it."

"The old broad is crazy. She's some do-gooder who should stay out of our business," Echo Trout replied hotly.

"I think she's on to something. I think Reynolds discovered why the three of you want Tex so bad," Grant said, his temper flaring. "I think something valuable is on that second chip, and one of you three injected it into Tex to hide it. That's why you've done all these crazy things in order to get that bull. You want him in order to get that chip."

"Do we?" Jimmy J asked, flourishing his cigarette in the air. "Why would I want that stinky bull?"

Grant appealed to his cousins. "He's lying, but you are my kin. Tell me the truth. Why do you want Dad's animals?"

Jimmy J exhaled a cloud of cigarette smoke and let out a wicked laugh. "You must be doing peyote, man."

Echo sat passively in a chair, not looking at his older cousin.

Glancing back and forth between Jimmy J and Grant, Narcy said, "We want to start our own breeding program. That's why."

Grant scoffed. "What do the two of you know about breeding rare livestock?"

"Your dad was teaching us. You were of no help to him," accused Narcy.

Grant said, heatedly, "It takes money to breed rare livestock. They have special needs. If you were helping Dad, I sure didn't see any sign of it. The place was a mess."

Echo offered an excuse. "After your dad's stroke, he wouldn't let us help. He got real paranoid."

"Now, Echo, how could you have been of any help to my father when you were living in Florida? You must think me stupid, cousin."

"Narcy was learning and going to cut me in after Uncle Ulysses died. He promised the farm to her. Isn't that right, sister?"

Narcy wiped her nose while nodding. "Echo's right, Cary."

"I wouldn't believe any of you even if you told me the sun was yellow. What do those chips have on them? Tell me now. Narcy? Echo? My father helped you both out many a time. You owe him something."

Bored with the family chatter, Jimmy J offered, "Maybe I should have a talk with this Reynolds woman? Straighten her out but good."

I bit my tongue to keep from laughing. Obviously, Jimmy J hadn't related to his compatriots that he had been ridiculed and chased from the farmers' market last Saturday.

Narcy quarreled, "You stay away from Josiah Reynolds, or they'll lock me up for sure, Jimmy. I'm in enough trouble."

"Then maybe you shouldn't hit people over the head when there are witnesses about," Jimmy remarked, taking a deep draw on his cigarette.

"What about this chip?" Grant asked, his voice rising higher. "I've heard rumors about drugs floating about. Was there some sort of drug information on that second chip?"

Echo answered, "We don't know anything about it."

"You're lying, Echo. I can tell when you're lying."

"You were always such a bully, Cary."

"And you, Echo, were always such a loser like your mother."

There was a sound of a scuffle with Narcy crying, "Stop. STOP! This is getting us nowhere."

Finally alarmed, Jimmy J said, "Look, Cary. I admit it. We need to get our hands on that chip. Where is it?"

Grant gave a bitter laugh. "Too late. The Reynolds woman gave the chip info to the police."

I heard boots stomp the floor with Jimmy J saying, "You're joking. I've got to have that chip." Anxiety had crept into his voice.

"That's what she told me not more than an hour

ago. It won't be long until the police come to pick you up. I know you had something to do with my father's death. I'm gonna help them every way I can. I'm gonna see you three fry for my father's murder."

"You can't prove nothing," sneered Jimmy J. "Your old man was gored to death by that deranged Long-horn."

"I found an old cattle horn hidden in the heat regis-ter at my daddy's office. That's my business—heating and air-conditioning. I know when something doesn't sound right coming out of a vent. I pulled it out and it had blood on it. I think it might have fingerprints on it as well."

"You better shut-up, old man," Jimmy J warned. "You're treading too far into dark waters."

Narcy turned toward Jimmy J and screeched, "Did you kill my uncle, you dirt bag? It's one thing to launder drug money through my uncle's business, but I'm not going to prison for murder."

"You are in too deep, Narcy. The old man got too greedy. Wanted a bigger cut."

Grant gasped, "So you did kill my father!"

"What of it?"

"Did you help him, Echo?"

Echo was sweating and pointed at his sister. "I was in Florida when your father died. I can prove it. If your father was murdered, I had nothing to do with it. Narcy's the crazy one. Ask her."

Cary shouted, "Narcy? Did you? Tell me the truth?"

Worried that her cousin might attack her, Narcy spoke quickly in a hysterical tone of voice, "I knew Jimmy J was going to have it out with Uncle Ulysses because we felt he was skimming off the top, but I swear I thought Tex gored the old coot. He was always so hard on that bull. Tex didn't like him and was hard to handle. Frustrated your father. I thought Uncle Ulysses hit him once too many times and Tex had enough. I swear, Cary. I swear it on the Bible."

"As if you have ever read the Bible. I'm gonna get the police. You three are going to jail."

"No, we are not, Cary," warned Jimmy J.

I heard a rushing of feet and fisticuffs. Narcy screamed. Oh, how I wished I could see what was going on. I looked around for something to stand on and peek in the window, but realized those days were over—no climbing on boxes in my present physical decline. I need a railing or fence post to hold onto when climbing.

"Put that gun away, Jimmy. It's over. Can't you see that?" Grant cautioned, his voice tremulous.

Jimmy J snarled, "Narcy and Echo will never testify against me as they are accessories after the fact. They are in it as deep as I am. It's you who's the problem, Cary."

"Listen Jimmy, put the gun away," Narcy begged. "Go now and leave the state. We'll keep Cary here overnight giving you time to get away. We'll tie him up."

"Leave this blabber mouth alive? No way."

Narcy implored, "Listen. If the police have the chip information, it's only a matter of time, Jimmy. Leave while you can. Please."

There was a shuffling of boots scraping across the floor, grunting, and sounds of a scuffle. Then a gun went off. BOOM! Then again another explosion of a gun. BOOM!

I was so startled, I almost dropped my phone.

Narcy screamed again as the front door slammed open against the side of the house.

Hearing boots scrap on the little stoop, I knew it was Jimmy J leaving the house. If Jimmy J saw me, I believed he would kill me for sure. So I ran and ducked behind the back of the doublewide to wait. A few seconds later I heard the squeal of Jimmy J's muscle car as it tore down the street.

There was a low wailing from Narcy and sounds of something being dragged across the floor.

I dialed 911 with trembling fingers.

The screen door opened again, and two people rushed down the small flight of steps, scurrying into a car which soon took off.

That left only me and whoever was left inside the trailer. As soon as I heard the second car peel off, I made my way to the front of the mobile home and climbed the steps to the small platform where the front door stood wide open. "Don't shoot," I called out. "It's Josiah Reynolds." I had been shot at before and didn't want to repeat the experience.

I gingerly stepped inside the trailer and caught sight of Cary Grant lying on the floor, injured. I bent over and felt for a pulse, discovering he was still breathing. Grabbing two dishtowels, I pressed them against the wound in his shoulder front and back.

"Oh, I'm gonna die. I'm gonna die," he moaned.

"Oh, stop whining," I said. "The bullet went through flesh. Didn't hit any bones. You're gonna be fine."

Wheezing, he flipped over from his side to sit on his bottom, leaning his back against the couch. "You're all kindness," he muttered, bitterly.

"I'm not the one who shot you."

He grabbed at my hand. "Did you set me up?"

I confessed, "Not to be shot, but I did set you up."

Grant winced. "I'm in pain. I need a doctor—now."

"Be grateful the bullet didn't ricochet inside your body. Went clean through. You'll be out of the hospital in a few days. Lucky."

"I don't feel lucky." Grant's hand dropped to his side. "What are you doing here, anyway?"

It was concerning that Grant didn't remember asking me this before. "Like I said—I set you up. I followed you here."

"You crazy . . ."

"Ah, none of that. Be nice to me since I heard everything. I'm a valuable witness."

The man's eyes brightened. "You did?"

"Not only that, but I recorded it. Even Jimmy J's confession that he murdered your father."

Grant closed his eyes.

Shaking him, I snapped, "Hey, open those eyes, Cary. Stay awake."

"I'm here. Don't shake me anymore, woman. It hurts."

I gave a ghost of a smile, not entirely sympathetic that this man was in pain. "Since you are at my mercy, so to speak, now would be a good time to agree that you will give me your father's animals."

Shifting his weight to a more comfortable position, Grant asked, "How can you speak about this now? I'm bleeding to death."

"No, you're not. Gosh, what a baby." I reached over and grabbed a pillow for his head before putting pressure back on his wounds. "That's why you decided to keep them, isn't it? You were suspicious of Echo and Narcy Trout."

"I was. I couldn't understand their sudden interest in livestock. I really don't want the animals. You can have the entire bunch, but one thing—tell me what really happened. Why did Jimmy J kill my father? He was a sick, old man."

"It was as Jimmy J said. Your father had a stroke and your cousins took advantage of that. Probably told your father that Jimmy J was a legitimate investor, but wanted to keep it quiet. I'm sure Echo and Narcy were sending out drugs and money under the pretense of selling Tex's semen which was being shipped to other drug dealers working for Jimmy J posing as livestock customers. I wouldn't believe Echo's story that he was in Florida when your dad died."

Grant seemed relieved. "Do you think my father understood what was going on?"

"I don't know. He may have been duped. I guess we'll never really know what the argument with Jimmy J was about. Your father might have threatened to call the police. Jimmy J lost his temper and shot him. Seeing Tex as a scapegoat, he found that old horn and pierced your dad's body with it to cover up the bullet wound."

"Detective McCain told me that there was more than one bullet discovered."

"Maybe your old man fought back and the gun went off several times. That would explain why Tex ran off. He was scared to death. I don't know much about cattle, but they don't like the sound of thunder or guns."

"No, they don't," Grant chuckled and then winced. "Oh, that hurts. You're pressing too hard."

We both turned our heads when we heard sirens.

"I'd like to think my father was clean and didn't understand what was happening with all this drug business." Grant sighed. "I should have kept a closer eye on him."

I didn't reply.

When tragedy happens, the survivor always plays the "should have" or "could have" game. I've learned regret is a waste of time. The only way forward is to push onward and shove the past behind.

Only life is not that simple. Is it?

34

Grateful that I helped him after being wounded, Cary Grant granted me title to his father's animals in exchange for not having to pay for their upkeep and my property damage. I was so sick of the entire episode with the Ulysses Grant melodrama, I agreed. Afterward, Cary Grant closed the breeding facility and sold the farm to a developer—more Bluegrass prime land to be bulldozed over. It is estimated that over 3200 Kentucky farms will be lost to development by 2040— some of the richest farmland in the world paved over. Isn't that depressing?

I still saw Cary from time to time when we were called to testify at Echo's and Narcy Trout's trials. They were tried separately for accessory to murder, money laundering, resisting arrest, and animal abuse to name a few charges.

Trying not to gloat as I passed the defense table on the way to the witness stand, I testified about the threats, Narcy's attack on me at the farmers' market, the attempt to steal the animals, trespassing, and my recording of the conversation at Narcy's trailer.

Franklin could never break the code on the chip and neither could the police when they got their hands on it. Last I heard the chip had been sent to the FBI lab, and they couldn't break it either. They said it was an encrypted sequence of numbers. Since the chip couldn't be tied to either the Trouts or Jimmy J, it was never admitted as evidence. Whatever it was, it was undoubtedly linked to a big-time drug cartel. It remains an enigma.

Detective McCain got a promotion and always strutted into the courtroom like a bellicose rooster. Annoyed that I got better press for solving the case, Lucas McCain said a few choice words to me in the courthouse hallway after I testified at Echo's trial. I reminded him that his handwriting expert almost brought about a miscarriage of justice when he deemed the Trouts' will authentic. It took Cary Grant to hire his own handwriting expert and lawyer to verify that will was a fraud. McCain had also missed the bullet holes, and it was Cary Grant who found the bull horn that gored his father. That shut Detective McCain down quick.

After my testimony, I didn't go back for the sentencing phase of the Trouts' trials. I read later that both Echo and Narcy Trout pled out to lesser charges before the juries reached a decision. They are still going to prison for years. The murder charge for Ulysses Grant was dropped because my recording proved they had nothing to do with it, but the attempted murder charge for Cary Grant stuck as well as money laundering, trespassing, forgery, and attempting to steal their uncle's animals.

I still have headaches from Narcy whacking me over the head.

Jimmy J was never caught. His red muscle car was discovered in flames at the Kentucky-Tennessee border, and he is thought to have fled the country.

35

As for the animals—well—they followed different paths. I loaned the Valais Blacknose sheep to two middle-school girls for their 4-H projects as Lady Elsmere suggested. They are not allowed to sell them and must return the sheep to me when they go to college. I visited both girls after several months to see if the sheep were in good health. I found the sheep fat and spoiled as pets with all their needs being met. I felt I left them in good hands. Checked them off my list.

I kept the shaggy, loveable Highland cattle because they are endearing. They are hardy, friendly beasts, and I like to stop by their pasture to gaze at them. It gives me pleasure to see them every day and I had the room, so they stayed.

I kept the Rove goats as well. My neighbors borrow them to eat scrub brush on their land. It's a win-win for my neighbors, and the goats seem happy to oblige.

I loaned the Belgian Blue bull along with the cow and calf to the University of Kentucky College of

Agriculture for study as long as the three were kept with each other. The dean of the department assured me that the plan was to partner with the French Livestock Institute for research into animal husbandry. Because I still own the Belgian Blues, the university sends me updates of their keep. If I don't like what I see, I will reappropriate the Blues. I've already made a surprise visit to their farm and found they were doing fine.

As for Tex and his ladylove, I found a Texas Longhorn sanctuary in Oklahoma that took them in. They have a herd of three hundred Longhorns, and their goal is to keep the breed alive and well.

"This is it, Tex. Your last apple from me." I pushed the apple through the fence and felt the bull's teeth scrape my hand as he snatched the apple. Overcome with emotion, I rubbed his snout as tears rimmed my eyes. I hated to see him go, but Velvet told me that he was not happy. He wanted to be with a herd.

Tex nudged my hand for another apple.

"Are you ready?" Velvet Maddox asked.

I nodded. "Let's hurry this up."

Velvet went inside the pasture where we had placed a trailer. She gently laid a trail of food down leading into the trailer with Tex moseying behind her. It took Tex a while to slowly munch his way inside but he finally made it. Once he was inside, the cow naturally followed. When the driver and assistant closed the back of the trailer and locked it, Tex immediately bellowed enraged.

Velvet grabbed my hand when I began to object. "Don't worry, Josiah. They'll both be fine. Tomorrow evening they will be at the sanctuary with their own kind, living their days in peace. Let them go and be happy for them."

I nodded and opened the gate for the truck and trailer. I didn't watch the truck pull out on the road.

Matt stood by the fence holding Emmeline, who was waving bye-bye to the truck. Seeing my stricken face, Matt asked, "Would you ladies like a nice glass of bourbon at my place?"

"Can you make a Kentucky Mule?" Velvet asked.

"Does the sun rise in the morning? You bet. I've got all the fixings."

"Then I'm your woman."

Matt asked me, "You coming, Josiah?"

"In a minute. You have that drink ready for me."

"Okay, but don't be too long. I need to put Emmeline down for her nap."

"Sure."

Tex was the last checkmark off my list. I should have been glad that he was gone, but I felt remorse—a sense of loss. I already missed the sight of those magnificent horns and his particular raunchy musk. Maybe I had been a rancher in another life.

The Longhorn was gone and I felt bereft. Who

knows why humans get attached to particular animals? I just know that Tex was special, and I was going to miss him.

And I did.

36

I never discovered why Esau Clay changed his tune about Tex and he has not offered an explanation or even an apology. When Esau sees me at social events, he slinks away or ignores making eye contact. There's a story there, but dang if I know what it is. Since I don't trust Esau anymore, I hired another vet. Sooner or later, Lady Elsmere will get to the bottom of Esau's story since she has contacts throughout the Bluegrass. Someone will feed her the story behind Esau and the Grants. I just have to wait for her to tell it to me.

After paying Shaneika Mary Todd and repairing the fence/barn/gate, I was in the low five figures, so yeah, I think Esau is a creep.

Taking a deep breath and letting go of some of my anger, I looked for Baby who I found in the stable playing with his cats. Hearing me call, he reluctantly came to me with a kitty perched on his back. "I see that you are giving the cats rides again."

Baby shook, causing the cat to jump off. "Food,

fellowship, and drink await us, Baby. Let's hurry to Matt's."

Baby nudged my hand for a friendly pat, which I happily obliged and realized I was happy. Walking with my best animal friend, we made our way to Matt's, my best human friend, so I ask you—wasn't I a woman rich beyond my wildest dreams?

Until next time.

Signing off.

Yours truly, Josiah Reynolds.

You're not finished. Keep going for the next Josiah
Reynolds Mystery!

Josiah is happy for her pals Lady Elsmere and Shaneika Mary Todd when broodmare Jean Harlow give birth to a male foal sired by Comanche. Both owners of the horses have high hopes the foal will become a stakes winner—maybe even win the Kentucky Derby. The foal has a broad chest, indicating significant lung capacity—important for winning races, but just like his daddy, the foal is ebony with a bad attitude.

Josiah and Shaneika visit dam Jean Harlow early one morning and are shocked to find the prized foal is missing. They frantically search Lady Elsmere's and Josiah's farms without success. It's urgent they find the foal fast as he is not yet weaned and is too young to be separated from his mother.

Who would snatch the feisty foal from his mother's care? And equally important, why?

Books By Abigail Keam

Josiah Reynolds Mysteries

Mona Moon Mysteries

About The Author

Hi, I'm Abigail Keam. I write the award-winning *Josiah Reynolds Mystery Series* and the *1930s Mona Moon Mystery Series*. In addition, I write *The Princess Maura Tales* (Epic Fantasy) and the *Last Chance For Love Series* (Sweet Romance).

I am a professional beekeeper and have won awards for my honey from the Kentucky State Fair. I live in a metal house with my husband and various critters on a cliff overlooking the Kentucky River. I would love to hear from you, so please contact me. Until we meet again, dear friend, happy reading!

You can purchase books directly from my website:
www.abigailkeam.com

Printed in the USA
CPSIA information can be obtained
at www.ICGtesting.com
LVHW041328280224
773024LV00055B/1268